THE IMPORTANCE OF LOVE

Cork brought the luncheon to the table and the Viscount started to discuss the gardens with her. He was far too nervous to broach the subject of marriage so early in the conversation.

Eventually, as the meal drew to a close, he knew he would have to take his courage in both hands and ask the question burning inside him.

Clearing his throat, he said,

"I was wondering if you have had the opportunity to consider my proposal."

Luella put down her dessertspoon and could not meet his eyes.

He noticed that she seemed hesitant to speak and believed the worst.

"I have," she responded at last in her clear musical voice. "But after what I am about to tell you, you may wish to consider whether or not to withdraw it."

"*Never*," he cried, his brown eyes burning. "Why would I do such a thing?"

"Because," mumbled Luella quietly. "I was once engaged – to another."

The Viscount's heart was now beating so furiously it made his breathing difficult.

"Is that all?" he spluttered. "It is of no consequence – it does not present any impediment to our becoming engaged."

"But, I – I am second-hand goods."

"You mean – ?"

THE BARBARA CARTLAND PINK COLLECTION

Titles in this series

THE IMPORTANCE OF LOVE

BARBARA CARTLAND

Barbaracartland.com Ltd

"When I was asked at the age of twelve what was the [mos]t important thing in life, I answered immediately – [LO]VE. I am now ninety and I have never changed my view [and I] will never do so!

Barbara Cartland

THE BARBARA CARTLAND PINK COLLECTION

Barbara Cartland was the most prolific bestselling author in the history of the world. She was frequently in the Guinness Book of Records for writing more books in a year than any other living author. In fact her most amazing literary feat was when her publishers asked for more Barbara Cartland romances, she doubled her output from 10 books a year to over 20 books a year, when she was 77.

She went on writing continuously at this rate for 20 years and wrote her last book at the age of 97, thus completing 400 books between the ages of 77 and 97.

Her publishers finally could not keep up with this phenomenal output, so at her death she left 160 unpublished manuscripts, something again that no other author has ever achieved.

Now the exciting news is that these 160 original unpublished Barbara Cartland books are already being published and by Barbaracartland.com exclusively on the internet, as the international web is the best possible way of reaching so many Barbara Cartland readers around the world.

The 160 books are published monthly and will be numbered in sequence.

The series is called the Pink Collection as a tribute to Barbara Cartland whose favourite colour was pink and it became very much her trademark over the years.

The Barbara Cartland Pink Collection is published only on the internet. Log on to www.barbaracartland.com to find out how you can purchase the books monthly as they are published, and take out a subscription that will ensure that all subsequent editions are delivered to you by mail order to your home.

NEW

Barbaracartland.com is proud to announce the publication of ten new Audio Books for the first time as CDs. They are favourite Barbara Cartland stories read by well-known actors and actresses and each story extends to 4 or 5 CDs. The Audio Books are as follows :

The Patient Bridegroom	The Passion and the Flower
A Challenge of Hearts	Little White Doves of Love
A Train to Love	The Prince and the Pekinese
The Unbroken Dream	A King in Love
The Cruel Count	A Sign of Love

More Audio Books will be published in the future and the above titles can be purchased by logging on to the website www.barbaracartland.com or please write to the address below.

If you do not have access to a computer, you can write for information about the Barbara Cartland Pink Collection and the Barbara Cartland Audio Books to the following address :

Barbara Cartland.com Ltd.
Camfield Place,
Hatfield,
Hertfordshire AL9 6JE
United Kingdom.
Telephone: +44 (0)1707 642629
Fax: +44 (0)1707 663041

THE LATE DAM
BARBARA CARTL.

mos
LO
and

Barbara Cartland who sadly died in May 20 of nearly 99 was the world's most famous roma who wrote 723 books in her lifetime with world over 1 billion copies and her books were trans different languages.

As well as romantic novels, she wro biographies, 6 autobiographies, theatrical pl advice on life, love, vitamins and cookery. S time to be a political speaker and televisi personality.

She wrote her first book at the age of 21 called *Jigsaw*. It became an immediate bests 100,000 copies in hardback and was tran different languages. She wrote continuously life, writing bestsellers for an astonishing 7 books have always been immensely popular States, where in 1976 her current books were 2 in the B. Dalton bestsellers list, a feat r before or since by any author.

Barbara Cartland became a legend in h and will be best remembered for her wond novels, so loved by her millions of readers world.

Her books will always be treasured f message, her pure and innocent heroines, h and dashing heroes and above all her belief t love is more important than anything else in

CHAPTER ONE
1901

"Come, Aunt Edith," whispered Luella Ridgeway, as she watched the bell boy struggling with a pile of suitcases as they entered the lift. "We must make haste."

The bell boy grunted and shifted the case under his arm so that it was more comfortable. Why the English ladies were in such a hurry at this hour of the night was beyond him.

"Luella," asked the Countess of Ridgeway, as she squeezed into the lift alongside her. "Did you remember to pack your nightclothes that were underneath your pillow? I do hope you did not leave that lovely silk nightdress behind."

"It's in the brown case," sighed Luella as the lift slowly descended.

The lift doors opened and they found themselves in a lobby that was eerily quiet. There was only a night porter on duty and one desk clerk.

The Countess strode purposefully towards the desk and, in clear French, asked for their bill.

"You are leaving us, Madame la Comtesse?" enquired the clerk.

"We are and I would be obliged to you if you would refrain from answering any enquiries as to our whereabouts or our destination. We wish to travel in secret."

"*Bien sûr*, Madame la Comtesse," replied the Clerk, handing over their account.

The Countess stared at it through her lorgnette and then pulled out several high-denomination notes from her purse. Luella stood nervously behind her, looking around with eyes as uneasy as a frightened rabbit's.

"Aunt, I do hope that awful man is not about to come through those doors," she said with a great deal of agitation in her voice.

"Do not concern yourself," replied the Countess. "I heard him order a carriage to the casino just a few hours ago – he will be ages yet. He will play until his funds have run out."

"I do hope so," muttered Luella, brushing back a strand of fair hair that had escaped from her hat. Her pale-blue eyes were large and the pupils very dilated. Her bottom lip trembled in her sweet, heart-shaped face and she looked for the whole world like an ethereal waif, wafted to earth by the Gods themselves.

It was those unusual looks that had brought her trouble. Ever since she had encountered Frank Connolly in a hotel in Monte Carlo, he had proved to be a most difficult customer.

"It is always the same with these hard-up buccaneers," her aunt had said, when he had made Luella cry with his persistent and unwanted attentions. "He looks at you and as well as desperately wanting to own your beauty, all he can see is a fortune that will rescue him from his ignominy. He must know that you stand to inherit a very large sum, not to mention all my Scottish estates when I am gone."

"Oh, Aunt, do not even mention that! I don't care a fig for your money, although I must admit that I love your castle very much."

"And it will be yours one day," the Countess had replied.

And now, a month later, they had been forced to flee from hotel to hotel with Frank Connolly in hot pursuit.

Finally, after a terrible week in Paris where he had threatened to take his own life if Luella would not promise to marry him immediately, they had decided to head for England and return to their Scottish home in Perthshire.

Tucking her purse under her arm, Aunt Edith followed the bell boy out to the waiting carriage and the night porter ran to hold open the door for them.

"*Bon voyage*, Madame Comtesse, Mademoiselle Ridgeway," he said with a bow. "Will we see you again soon?"

"I should not have thought so," said the Countess haughtily. Then turning to the driver she spoke urgently, "*Depechez-vous, monsieur. La Gare Saint Lazare, s'il vous plait.*"

With both women and their luggage safely on board, the carriage sprang forward and Luella heaved a sigh of relief.

She knew that her aunt was right. Frank Connolly would be at the gaming tables long into the small hours of the morning by which time they would be on the boat train for Dover.

As they tore through the streets of Paris, she sat back in her seat and thought of Scotland.

It had been a year since she had last set foot on British soil and she was looking forward to her return.

"We shall not linger in Dover," said Aunt Edith, as they reached the station. "I know a discreet hotel in Hastings where we shall stay before we make our way to the West Country."

"The West Country!" cried Luella. "Are we not travelling to London to catch the Inverness train? I had been looking forward to shopping and sight-seeing."

"No," asserted the Countess quietly. "London is the first place that Connolly will come looking for us. No, we shall outfox him by detouring to Cornwall and then, from there, we shall travel North as soon as I feel that the coast is clear."

"Why Cornwall, Aunt?"

"I have a very dear friend who lives just outside Bude whom I have not seen in many years. I have already written to her saying to expect us. Frank Connolly is not an easy man to shake off – an obsessed man never is. I shall not rest until we are on the boat and I am certain he is not on board."

Upon arriving the driver opened the door for them and Luella saw a porter scurrying towards them with a trolley for their cases.

"Yes, the sooner we reach Calais, the better," she agreed, following their luggage. "I so hope we have now shaken off Frank Connolly for good!"

*

"Very well, Kennington – I'll see you."

The red-haired man with the neatly clipped moustache drew heavily on his cigar and held his cards close to his face as the smoke curled upwards. Opposite him, David, the Viscount Kennington, sighed and threw his cards down on the table.

"A pair of sevens," he said in disgust as his fellow player scooped up the pile of coins and notes from the centre of the table. "I'm out, old man."

"What, you are quitting?"

"I am afraid so, Chalmers," sighed Viscount Kennington, rising from his chair. He swept his hand over his thick black hair and stretched out his long muscular arms.

The tie around his neck remained loose as he gathered up the small pile of coins next to him. He stood up and retrieved his jacket from the back of the chair.

"Another night, maybe, your luck will be better," said Lord Chalmers.

"I have lost all heart for the card tables of late," replied the Viscount wearily.

"Nonsense, man. You have just had a bad run of luck that is all. You should try another game next time."

The Viscount smiled thinly and adjusted his necktie. It was two o'clock in the morning and he was tired. He hoped that his driver had not fallen asleep outside in Hanover Square.

"Goodbye, then, Kennington. Will I see you at the Reform next weekend? Bit of a beano with the Straffords – their son and heir is getting married."

"I will see. Goodnight, Chalmers."

"Goodnight, Kennington, and do not disappoint us! Strafford will be dashed upset if you do not put in an appearance."

The Viscount smiled at him through the cigar smoke and buttoned his jacket. He strode towards the exit with a lithe grace that pointed to a fondness for athletics in his youth.

At Cambridge he had been the star of the rugby team as well as a champion oarsman.

But those days were long gone, as was his passion for architecture that had taken him to the university in the first place.

Many of his tutors had hoped he would become a very successful architect, but since returning to London he had idled his time away in the gaming houses and gentlemen's clubs of the Capital.

There were so many distractions once the Season started – and then there was the Gaiety Theatre with its beautiful and available women.

The Viscount had disappointed his father by showing no signs of continuing the family line by entering into the state of marriage. In fact, he had done everything in his power to avoid it.

"I do not ascribe much importance to love," he had told his companions, one evening around the dining table at Lord Cheshunt's house. "One should take one's pleasures naturally. But marriage? It is for fools who have no choice in the matter."

There had been much sage nodding of heads around the table of assorted Lords, Earls and Baronets, all of whom had made 'good marriages', but who inevitably found amusement in the arms of women other than their wives.

Climbing into his carriage, the Viscount yawned and was glad that the journey from Hanover Square to South Audley Street would be a swift one. He longed for the comfort of his bed in the house that his modest income had bought him.

'If only Father had not decided to punish me,' he thought.

The Viscount felt upset that his father had effectively curtailed his hopes of renovating and remoulding a derelict property that Lord Chalmers had told him about.

After he had refused to marry the heiress to the Merriott fortune, his father had shown his displeasure by cutting his allowance and forbidding the Viscount's grandfather from intervening and supplementing his favourite grandson's income.

"Grandpapa has always been keen for me to resurrect my career in architecture and that house Chalmers mentioned would have been just the thing," he murmured out loud. "Perhaps I should pay him a visit tomorrow and see if I can persuade him to help me out. What Father does not know cannot hurt him!"

With hope dawning in his heart, he settled back in his carriage and allowed the rocking movement to lull him to sleep. By the time they arrived at South Audley Street, he felt happier than he had done in weeks.

*

The next morning, Hoskin, the Viscount's valet, shaved him and helped him dress.

"Will you be requiring breakfast, my Lord?"

"Not today, Hoskin. I intend to call upon my grandfather. Some hot coffee is all I need."

As soon as Hoskin had finished attending to him, the Viscount gulped down a cup of coffee and put on his hat and a light jacket as the weather was warm and fine.

His mind was very much on the property that Chalmers had told him was up for sale – an almost derelict, Jacobean mansion on the outskirts of Buckingham with plenty of land and a river running through it.

'This would give me the opportunity to prove to myself that I am still capable of producing wonderful and modern designs,' he told himself, as he tipped his hat to Lady Castleford who passed by in her open landau on her way to Hyde Park.

He quickened his pace as he approached Grosvenor Place.

'I do hope that Grandfather will be able to give me the funds I require,' he thought, striding swiftly along Grosvenor Crescent to the imposing house in the far corner of Belgrave Square.

He was soon ringing the ornate brass doorbell and waiting for Bates, his grandfather's butler, to open the door.

The heavy door swung open and Bates greeted him robustly.

"My Lord! His Grace will be delighted to see you. He is in the dining room having his breakfast. Shall I set out another place for you?"

"That would be excellent, Bates. Thank you."

He walked towards the dining room and entered without waiting for Bates to announce him. The Marquis of Alderberry was busy taking the top off his egg and sighing over a headline in the newspaper.

"David. How nice to see you," he exclaimed. "Bally nonsense, this Boer War," he added, indicating the newspaper in front of him. "It's all boiling up again."

The Viscount sighed,

"I have no interest in military matters. Some of my Cambridge chums are out there and they write to me saying the whole affair is beastly."

He sat down in the chair that Bates had pulled out for him.

His grandfather was fond of a large breakfast and as usual there was a tasty selection of dishes keeping hot on the buffet.

"What will you have, my Lord?"

"Kedgeree and toast, please, Bates."

"Now, to what do I owe this honour, young man? You do not usually grace me with your presence so early. I suspect that something, or someone, has precipitated this visit."

The Viscount laughed fondly.

"You are as sharp as ever, Grandfather. Yes, there is something I wish to discuss with you."

"Well, ask away," said the old man with a smile.

"Grandfather, I will be blunt. I need a considerable

sum of money to invest in a derelict property that I have been tipped off has just become available. My thoughts are that this is a project I could really throw myself into."

"You are thinking of putting to good use all your learning at Cambridge?"

"Yes, I have grown tired of my life and think it is time that I revived my interest in architecture. Teddy Chalmers says that the location is wonderful and there is a great deal of potential for a man with an entrepreneurial spirit."

"That is to be admired, David, and I am glad that you are keen to engage yourself on such a worthy project, but I am afraid that your father has tied my hands when it comes to releasing funds to you."

"I know he has said not to give me anything, but surely he cannot tell you what to do with your own money?" asked the Viscount forking over his kedgeree.

"My son is a very wilful and stubborn man. He has tied up my liquid assets and there is nowhere near the amount of cash available that you would need. I am sorry, David, if I could help you, I would. Your father is still very angry with you over that dashed Merriott girl."

The Viscount put down his fork, having lost all his appetite.

"*Father*," he hissed through gritted teeth. "He complains that I live a wasted life and then, when I seek to knuckle down and make a name for myself, he puts obstacles in my path."

"He will not bend, David, and I am so sorry I cannot help you. Is there anyone else you can ask?"

"Not for such a large sum, Grandfather. It would not be right. And the bank is under Father's sway and will not loan me such an amount. He has effectively handcuffed me until I agree to marry."

"That is a pity, David," sighed the Marquis. "I shall

speak with him on your behalf, but I would not hold out a great deal of hope that he might change his mind. Once set, even the Almighty himself could not budge him from his path!"

The Viscount drained his cup of coffee and threw down his napkin.

"It is such a shame and it will be a great opportunity missed," he said. "And now, I should leave you in peace. Is Grandmama in?"

"No, she is staying at friends in Brighton and will not be returning until later today."

"Then send her my love. I shall detain you no longer."

He rose and shook his grandfather's hand solemnly and Bates was ready waiting for him with his hat.

The Viscount decided to go for a stroll in Green Park and began to make his way towards Buckingham Palace, but he had not gone far when he saw none other than his father striding towards him.

Taking a deep breath, the Viscount prepared himself for the inevitable confrontation. Relations were very strained between father and son and he knew it would not be an easy encounter.

The Earl halted for a moment as he caught sight of his son coming towards him. He rolled up his newspaper with a decisive gesture and walked forwards with a grim expression upon his face.

"David," he said halting by him. "What are you doing here?"

"I have been to see Grandfather," he answered, waiting for the inevitable burst of anger.

His father did not disappoint him.

"You did *what*?" he raged, turning red in the face. "I told you to keep away from him with your begging bowl, you ingrate!"

"But, Father, I had hoped to resurrect my career as an architect and had found a property to show off my abilities to everyone – "

The Earl grabbed his son by the arm and began to frogmarch him back in the direction of Belgrave Square.

"Now you will come with me and apologise for bothering him."

"Father, I do wish you would not treat me like a child," pleaded the Viscount, as he shrugged off his father's grip.

He would be thirty at his next birthday, yet his father still behaved as if he was a ten-year-old. And, being an only child, he bore the brunt of his father's expectations and plans for the Kennington family.

'I wish Mama was still alive,' he thought, as he was led back to his grandfather's house. 'She always used to stand up for me.'

But his mother had died not long after he had graduated from Cambridge. She had fallen ill with typhoid after working with the poor in the East End of London and not being very strong, she succumbed to death within weeks of being infected.

They soon arrived back at the Marquis's house. Bates was shocked to see the Earl and the Viscount standing on the doorstep.

Without waiting for him to speak, the Earl barged his way past him with a resigned-looking Viscount following behind.

"Father!" he shouted. "Where are you?"

The old Marquis shuffled into the hall with his newspaper still in his hand. He looked as if he had only just finished his breakfast.

"David," he called, for the Earl's name was the same as his son's.

"Father, I was on my way to visit you when I found this miscreant in the street, sneaking away from your house. I have told him frequently not to bother you and I am most displeased that he has disobeyed me."

"David, if you will only listen to the boy. He has a chance to make something of himself and bring glory to the family name."

"Rubbish! He came seeking money for the gaming houses. Don't think I am such a fool that I do not know where he spends most of his time. You did not believe what he said, surely?"

"But, Father, what Grandfather says is true. Teddy Chalmers has tipped me off about an old place that could be just right to show off my skills."

"What a waste of time that would be! How you scraped through Cambridge is beyond me. And I have paid the price in more ways than one."

"David, I don't think we should be raking up the past again. The boy did not wish to marry the Merriott girl for good reasons."

"And I lost out on a great deal of money and a lucrative business partnership because he did not snap her up. The silly young fool! United our two families would have been the most powerful force in the land."

"But I did not wish to get married, Father."

"We are not put on this earth as the ruling class so that we may choose when and whom we marry," he snapped angrily. "There are more important considerations such as loyalty to one's family. Considerations that you appear to have forgotten in your selfish life."

"*Stop this*," cried the Marquis, quite clearly upset. "I will not have such words spoken in my house."

However, the Earl continued to rail against his son, becoming more and more agitated. He thrust his finger into the young man's chest repeatedly and ugly words spilled forth from his lips.

"*Stop!*" called the Marquis again weakly.

Bates noticed that his Master was turning a peculiar colour and appeared to be having difficulty in breathing. His face turned blue and he slowly sank to his knees.

As the Earl had his back to him, the first he realised that something was amiss was when the Viscount rushed to help Bates haul the old man to a nearby chair.

"Send someone for the doctor," yelled the Viscount, loosening his grandfather's necktie. "And make haste."

The Earl stood horrified in the hall. He could neither move nor speak.

"Grandfather! Can you hear me?"

The Viscount was kneeling down by the old man and patting his hand. The Marquis let out a long sigh and then expired.

"Grandfather. No! No! *No!*"

"You – have – killed him," muttered the Earl, falling back against the wall.

The Viscount laid his head on his dead grandfather's knee and stifled a sob.

He had been brought up to believe it was not manly to cry, but how could he not shed a tear when the man he loved and respected more than any other had just died?

"Get up, you fool!" shouted his father hoarsely. "You are making a spectacle of yourself crying like a weak girl."

The Viscount remained with the Marquis until the doctor arrived.

"I am so sorry, my Lord," he said, shaking his head. "I would suggest that you have the servants remove his body to his bedroom. I will drop in on the undertaker on the way back to my house and ask him to come at once."

"Thank you," replied the Viscount, choking back his emotions. "That is very kind of you."

"I shall have to go home and write out the death certificate and will have it delivered as soon as possible. The undertakers will need it."

"Of course, thank you, doctor."

The Viscount walked with him to the door and past his still-stunned father.

As he closed the door behind him, he turned to face the Earl.

"Father – "

"Don't speak to me and don't look at me," snarled the Earl in a tone of voice that sounded as hollow as it was dangerous. "You are no longer my son!"

"Father, you are upset – you do not know what you are saying."

The Earl's eyes glittered as he regarded the Viscount with a cold stare.

"You killed him. You and your selfishness," he screamed. "Get away from me!"

He pushed past his son and pulled open the front door with such force that it rebounded off the wall and almost hit him as he stood in the doorway.

"You have your grandfather's death on your conscience. I will never forgive you! *Never*, do you hear?"

With that he ran down the steps of the house and out on to the street.

It had begun to rain and he pulled his hat down over his eyes as he rushed off, leaving the distraught Viscount feeling empty and numb as he stared after him.

CHAPTER TWO

The passage from Calais to Dover was not a smooth one for Luella and her aunt. The sea pitched their ship mercilessly and as a result they were both seasick.

By the time that they had docked at Dover, Luella was very worried about the Countess – she was almost delirious.

"I think we had better stay in Dover tonight and forget about trying to make for Hastings," she said, as two sailors helped her aunt down the gangplank.

"No, we must press on. I am well enough to withstand a carriage ride."

Luella regarded her ashen face with concern. Although her aunt was hardly in her dotage, she had never seen her look so frail. It was as if she had aged overnight.

The sailors quickly found them a carriage that sported a team of fast horses and made certain that she was comfortable before they bade farewell.

"What kind gentlemen," murmured the Countess, as Luella tucked blankets around her knees.

Outside it promised to be another fine July day, but the Countess was shivering and needed the extra warmth.

Luella sipped at the cup of water the sailors had brought for her and clutched at her stomach. She was slowly feeling a little better, unlike her aunt who groaned as the carriage bumped its way along the road to Hastings.

It was late afternoon by the time they arrived at their destination and the Countess had been asleep for much of the journey.

Luella had tried to make her as comfortable as possible and the coachmen had been most considerate, bringing them a water bottle and some plain bread and butter. The Countess had not touched anything apart from a few sips of water. It was left to Luella to advise the coachmen of their final destination – the *George Hotel* in Battle, just outside Hastings.

It was an old coaching inn and at first Luella was concerned that it would not be to their liking. However, once inside, they were shown to a comfortable suite of rooms that overlooked Battle Abbey.

'Surely Frank Connolly will not find us here?' she said to herself, as she waited for the landlord to bring them something to eat. 'He would not think of looking somewhere so modest.'

The thought did occur to her that perhaps he may pass through, as most of the London-bound coaches stopped at the inn.

'But he would never dream of finding us here,' she mumbled, gazing out of the window at the Abbey. 'Even so, I feel in my bones that he has discovered we have left Paris and is even now in hot pursuit. I hope we can outwit him as I do not know what I would do if he was to find us.'

*

The days after the Marquis's undignified death were highly fraught for the Viscount. He attempted to visit his father to clear the air, only to be told by his butler that he was not at home, when the Viscount knew quite clearly that he was.

'He will have to face me at the funeral,' he told himself as he walked back to South Audley Street.

Halfway there, he changed his mind and made for Belgrave Square instead. His grandmother had returned from her visit to Brighton to the terrible news and had been inconsolable ever since.

It did not help that no one seemed to be able to tell her the precise circumstances that led her husband to collapse.

The servants maintained a wall of silence, having been drilled by the Earl to keep their mouths shut on the subject and the poor Marchioness was beside herself.

The Viscount knocked on the black-wreathed front door and waited for Bates.

"Good afternoon, my Lord," intoned the butler, as his sombre face appeared in the hall. The Viscount noticed that he was wearing a black armband.

"Good afternoon, Bates. Is Grandmama at home?"

"Yes, my Lord. She is in the library, please come this way."

The Marchioness was sitting in an armchair with a pile of papers on her knee. As soon as she saw her grandson, she set them down and rose to kiss him.

"David," she exclaimed, her red-rimmed eyes staring balefully up at him. "How nice of you to come."

"I hope you did not think I was deserting you, Grandmama, it is just that Father – "

"Yes, I know. You two are still at loggerheads."

"I am sorry, I have tried to see him to smooth the way, but he has instructed his servants not to let me past the front door. It is very hurtful to be kept on the step like an unwelcome visitor."

"Your father always was a stubborn child and he grew up to become a stubborn man. He would rather die than admit he was in the wrong and as for apologising – "

"I came to see how you are."

The old lady sighed heavily and waved her hand at the piles of papers everywhere.

"As you can see, your grandfather left a great deal of unfinished business. His Solicitor has promised to call and help me attend to things, but I do not know what I shall do."

Her lip trembled and she dabbed at her eyes with a black-edged handkerchief. After a few moments she composed herself and looked up at him.

"David, you were here – will you tell me what happened?"

"I am not certain I should," replied the Viscount wearily. "If I did, then Father would use it against me and make me suffer even more."

"I am asking you, dearest, if there is something I should know."

"Very well. There was an argument between Father and me and Grandpapa became upset. The next thing we knew, he had slumped to the floor, clutching his chest."

The Marchioness contemplated his words for a while and then spoke,

"Thank you, David. I had suspected as much. You do know that your grandfather always had a weak heart? It was a miracle that he survived as long as he did. His doctors told us years ago that the end was in sight."

"You do not blame me?"

"For your grandfather's death? *No*," she shook her head. "The slightest amount of strain could have brought on a heart attack – one of his horses not winning the Derby, news that his investments had hit rock bottom."

He seized his grandmother's hand and kissed it.

"Thank you, Grandmama. Father blames me, of course. That is why he will not see me."

"He is a very stupid man, even if he is my son. You

are his only child and should be comforting him at this dreadful time."

"As long as you do not bear me any ill will, Grandmama, I believe I can bear his ostracising me."

"He will come round, just give him time. He always has to have someone to lash out at and this time it is you. Stay strong, David. We shall all need you very much at the funeral tomorrow."

"The Solicitor says it will be held at Kensal Green and not at the family Church in Hertfordshire. That is strange, is it not?"

The Marchioness took a deep breath and he could see that something else was troubling her.

"They were his last wishes and being a loyal wife, I do not wish to disobcy my husband, even in death. Now, if you will excuse me, David."

Tears were flowing freely down her face much to the Viscount's discomfort.

'There is something she is not telling me,' he thought, as he took his hat from Bates and left the house with its shuttered front windows.

*

Even before he left his home the next day for the funeral, the Viscount had a distinct sense of unease.

The cortege was to leave from Belgrave Square at eleven o'clock and the funeral was to be followed by the reading of the will at the Solicitor's office.

Arriving at his grandfather's house, the Viscount went to take his place with the chief mourners and was told that he should travel in one of the many carriages arranged for the journey to Kensal Green. Stung, he tried not to show how upset he was by this slight.

He could see his father from a distance, but he was

making a point of ignoring him.

At last, the undertaker announced that it was time to leave.

The Viscount looked at the velvet-draped coffin in the enormous, glass-bodied hearse festooned with a forest of black plumes and wanted to weep.

It took all of his inner strength not to sob aloud in front of the assembled throng.

Slowly, the undertaker took up his position in front of the team of six black horses. The procession began to move forward with the Marchioness and the Earl travelling in a black landau immediately behind the hearse.

Two outriders on liveried horses, a pair of feathermen and numerous pages all dressed in black with black streamers flying from their hats began the solemn journey around Belgrave Square.

On the side of the hearse were shields bearing the Marquis's coat of arms, topped with coronets, while the lavish fittings would have been considered eye-popping had they not graced a funeral vehicle.

The Viscount's carriage followed the parade. People from streets around lined the pavements to gawp at the spectacle.

At Hyde Park Corner, the undertaker jumped up onto the box of the hearse and the whole procession picked up speed as it made its way towards North Kensington.

Along the way, people stopped to doff their caps and bow their heads as a mark of respect. It had been a while since London had seen a funeral on such a grand scale.

Some time later they arrived at Kensal Green. After a short service in the Chapel, where many mourners were forced to stand outside, the coffin made its way to its last resting place.

The Viscount barely noticed the architecture of the solid mausoleum that rose up in front of them. It stood not two hundred yards from the famous tomb of Princess Sophia and, apart from the solid columns that flanked the four corners of the structure, it struck him as a rather modest affair.

In fact, he almost felt proud of the fact that his grandfather had chosen such a restrained monument.

For the older generation building an ostentatious and expensive final resting place had been all the rage during the early days of the *Belgravia of Death* as Kensal Green had been named.

Yet here was one of the most important and aristocratic men in the Kingdom about to be interred in a building that would have been self-effacing for a merchant, let alone a Marquis.

'Oh, Father. Do not ignore me,' thought the Viscount, as the pain in his heart increased. Each time he attempted to catch his father's eye, the Earl simply looked away. 'Why must you make everything so difficult?'

The Minister began to intone the final rites as the pallbearers halted by the open door.

With tears in his eyes, the Viscount's gaze rested upon the lintel over the door that bore a name. Squinting he began to make out the letters of the name.

"*Le Fevre*," it read.

'Le Fevre?' thought the Viscount.

Moving swiftly to the side of the mausoleum, he pushed through the crowds to read the simple inscription.

"*My well-beloved, Marie-Annette Le Fevre, taken from this world 26th January 1891.*"

Underneath the inscription was a carving of an angel next to a dove carrying a streamer in its beak to Heaven.

The meaning was quite clear to the Viscount. This was a woman whom his grandfather had quite clearly adored! And what was more –

'It was not my Grandmama,' he breathed almost audibly.

Perplexed, he returned to where he had first been standing. His head was whirling and he felt a little unsteady on his feet.

Reaching out to anchor himself, he touched the shoulder of one of his younger cousins who turned round to face him with a face like a frightened whippet.

"David," she chided in an undertone. "What ails you?"

"I am sorry, Arabella," he replied, a wave of nausea sweeping over him and a clammy sweat breaking out on his brow. "I suddenly felt a little dizzy."

"Poor David," she whispered. "You and Grandpapa were very close, were you not? It must be dreadful for you."

Someone in the crowd hissed at them to hold their tongues and the sound of the bell tolling drowned out the rasping sound.

The coffin was now being laid to rest on the stone shelf inside the mausoleum.

The Viscount did not enter to stand alongside his grandmother and father. He remained a little way from the entrance, wondering who on earth Marie-Annette Le Fevre had been and why she so occupied a place in his grandfather's affections that he had risked a terrible scandal by being buried alongside her.

The Viscount knew that it would soon be the talk of London and that the family name would now be covered with infamy.

At last the ceremony drew to a close. The furious

waggling of black funeral bonnets told the Viscount that he was not the only one to have noticed the name on the side of the mausoleum.

'That is why Grandmama was so upset yesterday,' he thought, as he returned to his carriage.

He instructed the driver to wait a while until the crowd had dispersed and then charged him to make all haste to Holborn.

*

The *George Inn* remained a sanctuary for Luella and the Countess over the course of the next few days. The Countess's health did not improve and gave Luella cause for great concern.

The Landlord was kind enough to send for a local doctor, who did his best, but seemed more interested in getting downstairs and filling his tankard than alleviating Aunt Edith's condition.

Luella wished there was a friend she could send for, but they were all miles away in Scotland.

And the omnipresent threat of Frank Connolly hung like a long shadow over her.

As a result, she only ventured out when absolutely necessary and spent her days reading in the tiny sitting room that adjoined their bedrooms.

Then one afternoon whilst staring out of the window, she was staggered to see Aunt Edith standing rather shakily in the doorway.

"Aunt Edith. What are you doing out of bed?"

"It's no good, Luella. I cannot bear being in it a moment longer. Would you ask the landlord to bring me a boiled egg? Then you must charge him with finding us a carriage West."

"Surely you are not thinking of continuing our

journey?" exclaimed Luella horrified.

"We have been here long enough and I promised myself that as soon as I was strong enough to stand, we would leave."

Nothing Luella could say would dissuade her from her intended course. Reluctantly, she went downstairs and requested the egg and ordered a carriage West.

As she returned to their rooms, Luella shook her head in exasperation.

'If anything happens to Aunt Edith, I shall only blame myself,' she said to herself wearily trudging upstairs. 'I would almost sooner face Frank Connolly than have her kill herself on my behalf!'

*

The Earl's carriage was already outside the Solicitor's office by the time the Viscount arrived.

As he climbed down, a motor car whizzed past and almost ran him over. Just in time, he heard the honking of the horn and jumped out of the way.

"Goodness! That was close," he cried, as he watched the motor car disappear in a cloud of dust.

He mused that the streets of London were now filling up with these mechanical monsters.

In fact he had considered purchasing one himself from the showroom in Berkeley Square. That was, of course, before his father had cut his allowance to a bare minimum. Now, it was all he could do to pay the servants' wages.

They were all waiting for him inside Mr. Brownlow's large office. His father sat furthest away from the door with a face like a sphinx, while his grandmother tried to raise a smile for him, but it appeared more like a grimace.

Also in the room were a few distant relatives whom the Viscount only ever saw at family gatherings.

'Vultures,' he thought, as he acknowledged them.

"Are we all present now?" asked Mr. Brownlow. "My Lord?"

"You may begin, Mr. Brownlow," said the Earl without a hint of emotion.

He adjusted his spectacles, took a deep breath and began to read,

"To my son, David, I bequeath the house in Belgrave Square, the house in Chalfont and the bulk of my fortune, subject to the condition that my wife, Emmeline, is allowed to live in it and be kept by him until the end of her days."

The Earl gave a slight nod as if satisfied and moved to rise.

"If you please, my Lord, there is more – "

The Earl looked at the Solicitor with a quizzical lift of his eyebrows.

"More?"

"Yes, my Lord. May I continue?"

"Of course."

"To my grandson, David, I bequeath Torr House in Bideford, North Devon, along with a stipend to be used solely to renovate the property and to make it once more the most splendid and beautiful house in the area."

"What house is this?" cried the Earl, before the Viscount had a chance to make further enquiries. "I know of no house in Devon!"

He jumped to his feet and hovered dangerously close to Mr. Brownlow's desk.

"It is, erhem, *was* your father's property. Look, I have the deeds here."

Mr. Brownlow produced a parchment covered in gothic script. The Earl took it from him as if he did not believe of its existence. After reading a few lines, he threw it across the desk.

"What is it, David?" asked the Marchioness. "If it is to do with *that woman*, then I wish to be informed."

There was such a tense silence in the room that no one dared moved a muscle.

"Would everyone leave now please, apart from my son and my mother," said the Earl through gritted teeth.

"*Well*," came the exclamation from one of the cousins.

The Viscount had a sinking feeling he knew who the house had belonged to.

When he was a child, his grandfather had often declared himself off to the West Country for the shooting or the hunting and reappearing weeks later.

He had never questioned the reason for his grandfather's long absences as so many of the nobility emptied out of London during the pheasant season or for Whit Sunday. Was it not all part of the Season?

And now it all became horribly clear to him.

'Grandpapa had kept a mistress,' he reasoned, as Mr. Brownlow closed the door behind the last of the relations.

Mr. Brownlow cleared his throat as the Earl glared at him.

"Would you mind explaining to us what this is about? I know of no house in Devon and the man *was* my own father."

He leaned over the desk at the Solicitor who appeared to be unruffled by this turn of events.

"Darling, sit down," said the Marchioness in a quiet voice. "It is quite all right, Mr. Brownlow. I was well aware of my husband's other life."

"Other life!" shouted the Earl. "What other life is this? And why did I know nothing of it?"

"Your father did not wish you to know. He thought it would be better if you did not."

"Mama, how can you sit there so calmly? The man was an adulterer and disgraced his wedding vows. And now this. Brownlow, there must be some mistake. Are you certain this house of shame was not meant to be sold and the profit given to me?"

"I am afraid that his Lordship was quite definite, my Lord. I witnessed the will myself. Torr House goes to your son, David."

"Outrageous!" screamed the Earl, waving his cane at the poor man. "Not only does my mother have to suffer the humiliation of having my father's grubby little secret aired to all and sundry at the funeral, but now his whore's house goes to my son. It should be sold, I say. And the memory wiped off from our family's slate."

"Not possible, my Lord. Unless, of course, Lord Kennington wishes to sell it. Although I must emphasis that should he do so, he will not inherit the money and, as the place is almost uninhabitable, he would not make much from it."

The Earl's eyes bulged with fury.

"Come along, Mother. We have heard enough," he fumed. "Brownlow, I shall contest this farce of a will. It has brought shame to our name and should be disposed of, along with that damned house."

He hoisted his tearful mother up from her chair and bundled her out of the door without so much as a backward look or a goodbye to Mr. Brownlow.

As the door slammed shut, the Viscount let out a sigh.

"I am sorry for my father's outburst. He is deeply upset, as we all are."

Mr. Brownlow nodded sagely and pursed his lips.

"Death does not bring out the best in people," he remarked. "But your grandfather was very definite about leaving the house to you. I know that he hoped you would make something brilliant out of it and resume your passion for architecture. That is why he left you this particular bequest."

The Viscount arose and shook Mr. Brownlow's hand. As he went to leave, the Solicitor called him back.

"My Lord, you will need these," he said, handing him a large bunch of keys. "You will find two servants in residence who keep the house open and they will be very glad to see you. Do not let them or your grandfather down."

Extending his gnarled hand, the Viscount shook it warmly.

Several moments later, he found himself standing on the pavement still clutching the heavy bunch of keys.

He turned them over in his hand. There were two large ones with ornate handles and several smaller ones. Their thick black iron was tinged with red rust that stained his pigskin gloves.

'Torr House,' he murmured, wondering what it looked like. 'Grandpapa, *I shall not let you down*. Even if the place is a ruin, I shall do your bidding.'

With one look up to Heaven, he choked back his emotions before walking purposefully towards his waiting carriage.

CHAPTER THREE

Once back home the Viscount sank into a mild depression that took several days to shake off.

He would sit for hours at a time, twirling the keys from Torr House in his hand and pondering his grandfather's bequest as he regarded the ageing metal.

Mr. Brownlow had sent him some correspondence after the reading of the will, giving him some more details of the house.

There were two servants, a butler, Cork, and a housekeeper, Mrs. Cork, who kept the place open, although he emphasised that they lived in a cottage in the grounds as the main house was in such desperate need of renovation.

"Your grandfather abandoned the house once Madame Le Fevre died and said he could not bear to visit it and be reminded of her," he wrote. *"As a result, only minimal repairs were carried out. The roof was patched five years ago after a storm caused damage, but that is all. You are to be given the sum of twenty-five thousand pounds initially with an annual income of five thousand pounds, subject to you taking up residence in the house for a period of no less than three months per year."*

'He must have loved this French woman very much,' thought the Viscount, as he ruminated on his grandfather's extra-marital domestic arrangements.

'But then again, it is highly likely that his and Grandmama's marriage was not a love match. With his being the heir to such a vast and powerful title, it would have been only natural for his parents to have sought a political alliance.'

His grandmother had been an Earl's daughter and the marriage of the two great and powerful families lent both sides considerable weight in the world at large. Although she had a brother, she had inherited all of her mother's property and fortune and that had enriched the family further.

But love?

The Viscount shook his head as he spoke aloud,

"Although Grandmama clearly loved Grandpapa, I was never certain that it was reciprocated. Respect and admiration, yes – but passion? No. He found that in this French woman's arms, that much is definite."

He put down Mr. Brownlow's letter and gazed out of the window of his study.

The small garden was blooming and he noted that the roses had done very well this year.

The thought that he might enjoy a garden but in a more beautiful setting made him come to a decision.

And then, there was the prospect of stamping his own mark on Torr House.

His thoughts were interrupted by Hoskin asking what he would like to wear to the dinner at the Reform Club that evening.

"I shall not be going," he said decisively. "Please begin packing my things. We are going to Devon."

"Devon, my Lord?"

"Yes, Hoskin. I want you to go downstairs and assemble the servants. I shall make an announcement in fifteen minutes. Tell them not to worry – no one is going to lose their job. I shall need every last pair of hands with what I have in mind."

The valet bowed and left the room.

The Viscount picked up Mr. Brownlow's letter once more and flicked through the deeds.

There was one photograph of the place, taken in the days when it had been the most important house in the area. The tall Jacobean chimney pots and tessellated windows gave it an air of ageing dignity, while the oak frame contrasted with the rich earthy-coloured bricks looked homely rather than grand.

'It should have been a house filled with children,' he mused, surprised at himself for thinking such a thought.

Setting down the photograph, he took up his sketchpad and quickly drew the outline of the house. Once that was completed, he sketched in a new wing to the left and an orangery to the right.

'It's a pity I do not have a rear elevation,' he was considering, as a knock on the door alerted him that Hoskin had returned to tell him that the servants were ready.

Getting up from his chair, he went out into the hall to impart his news.

"I shall require two servants to remain in London to look after this house," he said. "If anyone would care to volunteer, it would save me a great deal of anxiety."

The butler, Bellamy, and his wife the housekeeper, immediately stepped forward.

"Good, I was hoping you might offer. Now, we leave for Devon in a few days and you must have all your belongings ready to take with you. You will be travelling down to Devon by train and conveyed from the station to the house. Once I have more details, I shall inform you all."

They filed out of the hall to resume their duties. The

Viscount knew that the next few days would pass very quickly and he intended to set down as many ideas as he could.

'I will do as Grandpapa wished,' he vowed, as he gazed at the sepia photograph once more. 'I will make him proud of me, up in Heaven, even if my own father refuses to acknowledge I exist!'

*

The Viscount did make one further attempt to visit his father, but to no avail, but he did bump into his grandmother in the foyer at *Claridge's* taking afternoon tea and they sat and chatted.

"I am so sorry that things have become so strained between you and your father," she sighed. "I have tried to speak with him on several occasions, but he will not listen to me. He simply turns away or walks out of the room."

"As long as we are not openly arguing, Grandmama, I can bear his indifference."

"It is not indifference, dearest. He might not say a great deal, but he does still have feelings for you. Unfortunately, his stubborn streak will always win."

"Grandmama. I feel I should inform you that I intend to travel to Devon at the end of the week."

She stiffened in her seat and pursed her lips. Her tone, when she spoke, was measured, but he could not detect any hint of telling emotion in it.

"You must do as your grandfather desired," she answered calmly. "He would wish you to rekindle your love of architecture and it is the perfect project for you. It is also a means to an end as I know your father has cut your allowance again."

"Yes. I will be frank, Grandmama, if Grandpapa had not left me the money for this house and the allowance, I would be forced to sell South Audley Street and go and live at my Club. A gentleman may always get credit after all."

"You will do no such thing!" cried his grandmother. "If matters become so difficult, then you must come to me."

"I would not dream of it," he replied, placing his hand on hers. "Now, let me see you to your carriage. I have some rather pleasant business in Mayfair."

After escorting his grandmother to her carriage, the Viscount headed for the garage in the mews behind Berkeley Square to buy himself a motor car.

He had heard that the new King had been driven in a Daimler and wished to see one for himself.

In the *Westminster Gazette* he had seen just what he wanted and, once he had bought it, he followed up their recommendation for an agency that supplied chauffeurs and he called in on their offices in Maddox Street.

At the agency, the owner had been very pleased to see him and, within half an hour, had engaged a very cheerful fellow by the name of Bennett, who had recently driven the Duke of Edenbridge until the old man died.

With so much achieved in one afternoon, the Viscount returned home feeling very pleased with himself.

The motor car was delivered the day before they were due to leave for Devon. Bennett made himself extremely useful, helping with trunks and bags and even went to Paddington station to obtain the train tickets for the other servants.

"They will have to be ferried from Barnstaple to the house in Bideford as there is no local station," he told the Viscount. "Shall I make enquiries about a private carriage or two for them?"

"Of course. They cannot be expected to walk with all their luggage! Thank you so much, Bennett. Is the car ready for the long journey ahead?"

"It is, my Lord, and I have obtained a travelling map

from Stanford's for the journey. I suggest we stop at the *Angel Inn* in Salisbury for an overnight stay. We should not attempt the journey in one day."

"I had expected as much. They say these new motor cars are capable of travelling more swiftly than horses, but I have my doubts."

The house felt very strange and empty with all his furniture covered.

The next morning the Viscount saw off his servants on their way to Paddington and said his goodbyes to Bellamy and his wife.

Climbing into the passenger seat of his new car, he felt a little sad to be leaving the house he had lived in since he had left Cambridge.

'At least I had the opportunity to say farewell to Grandmama,' he thought, as the car rocketed forwards.

He held on to his hat as it gathered speed. Bennett was a smooth driver, but the gears on the new motor car seemed a trifle stiff.

They were soon driving through the West of London on the old coaching road to Exeter. Bennett had planned the journey to the last mile and intended to stop for luncheon at an inn outside Reading and then dinner at the *Angel Inn* in Salisbury.

"I have reserved two rooms for us, my Lord, as well as alerting them that we shall be bringing a motor vehicle and will not need stabling for the night."

"Excellent, Bennett. It is exhilarating travelling at such speed, is it not?"

"Oh, I have become used to it, my Lord. The old Duke used to like me to put my foot down on the accelerator to see what we could get out of the old girl. He used to cheer and wave his hat whenever we passed carriages."

The Viscount laughed.

"You must drive carefully – the roads will soon be rougher than in London and we do not want an accident. There is so much to go wrong on these things!"

"And a lot can ail a horse too, my Lord."

The day was warm and fine and the Viscount soon took off his goggles against the wind and fully enjoyed the scenery. The scattered villages of Middlesex soon gave way to the rolling hills of Berkshire.

The scenery began to flatten as they approached Salisbury Plain in the late afternoon. The Viscount could see for miles around and ordered a stop at Stonehenge so that he could see the stones at close range.

He thought of Thomas Hardy's book, *Tess of the d'Ubervilles* where the heroine had met her doom at the stone circle and, as he stood there with the wind whistling around his ears, he turned to face the West and wondered what lay in store for him.

It suddenly occurred to him that he would not know a soul apart from the servants and that any newcomer to the town would be viewed with suspicion.

'I shall do my best to be as popular as Grandpapa would have wished, that is all I can do,' he murmured, as he climbed back into the Daimler.

*

They arrived at the *Angel Inn* around seven o'clock.

While Bennett unloaded his luggage, the Viscount strolled around the stables.

He was pleased to notice that his was the only motor vehicle on the premises and took great pride in the fact that their arrival had caused something of a stir.

He spent a pleasant evening at the inn. Their fare was hearty, if simple, and the portions were large. He slept well in a feather four-poster bed and arose the next morning prepared for an early start.

Bennett had the motor car ready by half-past eight and they were on the road well before nine.

"I wonder if the staff have arrived in Barnstaple yet?" shouted the Viscount above the roar of the engine.

"I would have thought so, my Lord," replied Bennett. "Rum old business, there being no station at Bideford, though."

"Yes," grimaced the Viscount as a sheep, startled by the sound of the horn, leapt out of their way. "We cannot expect any of the comforts we enjoyed in London. They do not even have gas lights!"

"Goodness!" cried Bennett. "And I thought I had done with the days of candles."

"We shall be roughing it for a while, Bennett. You do not mind after such luxury at the Duke's house?"

"Not at all, my Lord. I was a stable hand when I was a young fellow and was used to sleeping in a hay loft above the horses."

The road through the top of Exmoor was rough and no more than a track for carts. The steep hills they encountered on the road to Barnstaple taxed the Daimler to its limits and the Viscount wondered how carts negotiated them.

It was getting dark by the time they reached flatter ground and a milestone on a crossroads that told them Bideford was only four miles away.

'I shall be glad of a respite from this boneshaker,' thought the Viscount, as the road followed alongside the river Torridge. Bennett had to stop once and ask a passing shepherd with his dog where they might find Torr House.

The man replied with a rich Devon burr that Bennett found quite difficult to follow.

"Lawks, they talk strange in these parts!" he exclaimed, shaking his head as the man wandered off.

But he must have understood at least part of what the shepherd had told him as the road from Eastleigh soon gave way to the outskirts of Bideford.

"We have to cross the bridge over the Torridge and the house can be seen from there, apparently, my Lord," said Bennett, as their motor car caused a great stir on the streets of the town.

A while later, they crossed the bridge and as the road curved round to the right, the house came into view.

The Viscount sat up in his seat and squinted into the distance.

Torr House nestled on the side of a hill with a long dusty drive leading up to it. His heart began to beat faster as they drew closer.

"This is it!" shouted Bennett, changing gear and slowing down by the gates.

The Viscount looked up the track, but could not see the house as, at that level, it was obscured by trees. He signalled to Bennett to move forward and the car made its bumpy way towards the house.

At last, as they passed the trees, Torr House sprang into view.

The Viscount caught his breath as he first set eyes on it. It had a faded beauty of its own, he thought. Although Bennett probably expressed the popular view when he blurted out,

"Lawks, it's a bit of a wreck, isn't it, my Lord?"

He turned off the engine and immediately a tall man with a sombre face emerged from the front door. Judging by his attire, the Viscount assumed he was Cork, the butler, who had served Madame Le Fevre for many years.

"Welcome to Torr House," he said, as his face broke into an unexpected smile. "I cannot tell you how glad I am you have come – and so is everyone in these parts. We all hope that you will rescue the place from wrack and ruin."

"It looks like I have arrived just in time," commented the Viscount, as he noted the peeling paint on the door and the latticed windows with panes missing and covered with brown paper to keep out the elements.

"This is Bennett, my chauffeur. Would you be kind enough to direct him to a dry place where he can park the Daimler?"

"That would be the barn, my Lord," replied Cork, his drawled vowels belying his Devon roots. "It doesn't have a door but it's dry enough."

With a bemused expression, Bennett unloaded the luggage and then drove the car round to the rear of the house as directed by Cork.

The Viscount was shown inside and immediately he fell in love with the place.

The hall was typical Jacobean with a hefty wooden staircase rising up solidly in front of him, while the walls were covered with oak panelling. What he thought was a cupboard door, turned out to be the entrance to the gunroom, while he looked at the large stag's head high looming over the stairwell.

"Is there hunting around here?" he asked, as Cork took him upstairs.

"The best in all of Devon, my Lord. The Exmoor hunt is the largest hereabouts and you'll find plenty of folk come down from London and Bristol for the sport. We even get some of them industrialists from up North."

"Really?" remarked the Viscount, astounded that this part of the country should boast such a thriving social scene.

"And then there's the pheasants in a month's time –

rich pickings for gentlemen like you."

"I had no idea – " began the Viscount, as Cork showed him into a large, draughty room with a dusty four-poster bed and heavy oak furniture.

"This was Madame's room, but I am certain she would not mind, that is, if you do not object considering – "

The words died on Cork's lips.

The Viscount nodded. He knew exactly what he meant.

'As long as I do not mind sleeping in my grandfather's mistress's bed,' he said to himself.

The fireplace was a large stone affair with a carving of a shield in the middle.

"How old is the house, Cork?"

"Three hundred years old or thereabouts. One of King James I's Scottish Lords built it when he was given lands in these parts."

The Viscount examined the faded silk curtains at the windows. Once a rich red they had been bleached pink by the years of sunshine. They were threadbare in places, as was the Turkish rug beneath his feet.

"I've aired the bed, my Lord, and I trust it will be comfortable for you."

It occurred to the Viscount that it might be damp. He moved over to it and threw back the red paisley quilt and examined the sheets for signs of mould.

"All appears as it should be, Cork," he said with relief.

"Dinner will be served at eight, my Lord. I hope that suits you?"

"It does, thank you."

"We have some fine local lamb and vegetables from the garden for tonight's meal. It is overgrown, but we manage to get by on what remains to be cropped. It used to be a beautiful place when Madame was alive, but it has become overgrown and neglected since she passed away."

"I intend to breathe new life into every part of this building," the Viscount announced looking up at the ceiling with its obvious signs of damp.

A large crack ran along the width of the room and the wooden chandelier contained burned-down stumps of candles.

"That is good news, indeed, my Lord. Now, when you are ready, shall I send Hoskin up to attend to you?"

"I would like that very much, thank you."

"When would you like to view the house, my Lord? Either myself or Mrs. Cork will show you around."

"I think before dinner. Then I will look around again in the morning."

"You are a draughtsman, are you, my Lord? We saw the drawing board being carried in and thought you might be an artist until we saw the size of it."

"I am an architect, or at least, I was. I intend to make this house magnificent again for all of Society to flock to."

"Madame would have liked that," smiled Cork enigmatically.

He bowed and left the room.

The Viscount's luggage was brought in and left for Hoskin to unpack.

As soon as he had finished, he drew the Viscount a bath with hot water in cans brought up by the maids who had arrived ahead of them.

"I hope your Lordship does not mind having to bathe in such an ancient vessel," remarked Hoskin, as the last of the hot water was poured into the huge enamel bath.

"I shall install modern bathrooms with running water as soon as possible. I shall investigate installing both heating and hot water. Tomorrow, I shall invite the builders to call. Have you a list of the local tradesmen for me as I requested?"

"Oh, yes, my Lord. Cork has been most helpful. He says that now word is out that you are to remodel the house, there will be no stopping them from calling on the off-chance of work."

"That is indeed good news."

The Viscount eased his body into the hot water and as he soaped his aching muscles his thick hair fell forward and soon became damp with suds.

Stretching out his long arms, he lay back in the water and closed his eyes.

'Already I can see what this house could be,' he told himself, 'and it shall rise from the ashes.'

Much later, after a delicious dinner, he retired early intending to sleep, but found it impossible.

He tossed and turned in the bed, which, although comfortable, was a strange one nevertheless. He resolved to bring his own bed from London, as he did not fancy sleeping on a mattress that had once borne his grandfather and his mistress.

As the house grew quiet, the room became chilly and he found himself still wide awake. Eventually, he climbed out of bed and put on his warm dressing gown.

Pacing the room, he became enthused with thoughts of how he might plan the house. He picked up his sketch book in which he had made a few drawings and looked at them again with the benefit of having now seen the house for himself.

'The orangery will not work there,' he muttered, striking it out on the sketch. 'And it might yet be possible to add another floor here.'

Before he knew it, he had picked up his pencil and was

busy redrawing the plan. He worked on and on through the night and did not notice the passing of time.

When Hoskin came in early the next morning with a tray, he was shocked to see his Master up and busy.

"My Lord. You look as if you haven't been to sleep."

"Indeed, I have not," replied the Viscount, wearily rubbing his face with one strong hand. "I could not sleep in that bed and once my mind began to form plans and designs for this place, I found I was too restless for slumber. And so, I got up and began to work.

"Hoskin, will you have my work things set up in the library for me after breakfast? I cannot work here indefinitely and will need a place to go where I will not be disturbed by maids."

"Of course, my Lord," replied Hoskin, handing him a cup of tea.

Later, after breakfast was over, the Viscount hurried eagerly into the library to begin work.

'It is a good deal shabbier than I had first thought. This is going to tax my ingenuity,' he murmured, as he sharpened his pencil and took out a fresh sheet of paper, feeling once more that familiar thrill of tackling a new design.

'But, yes, I think I shall be very happy here.'

And a slow smile spread across his handsome face as he began to draw.

*

"Are you certain we are heading in the right direction, driver?" asked Luella, as the carriage they had hired at Southampton began to climb uphill.

The Countess groaned and looked even paler than earlier that morning.

Luella had entreated her to stay awhile longer in

Southampton, but she would not hear of it. And now she was looking worse with each passing mile.

Furthermore, she was losing confidence in their driver to take them to their destination. He had been forced to turn the horses round once already as they had taken a wrong road, having passed through Okehampton, he had not heeded the sign to Bude and was now haring off in the direction of Great Torrington.

Although Luella did not have a map or a compass, she was concerned as she now believed they were heading due North. She had a good sense of direction and North was where Scotland and home lay. And now with the sun moving off to their left every fibre in her body was screaming that they were on the wrong road.

"Oh," moaned Aunt Edith, as the carriage hit a rock in the road and jolted.

"Aunt. Do you wish us to stop?"

The Countess nodded and Luella leaned out of the window and shouted to the driver to stop. She helped her aunt out for some fresh air.

As she stood quivering with nausea by the roadside, Luella was furious with the man. She put her aunt back inside and rounded on him.

"Do you actually know where we are?" she cried with her pale-blue eyes flashing dangerously.

The driver hung his head and mumbled,

"I's sorry, miss, but I don't know these 'ere parts."

"You said you knew the way to Bude."

"Sorry, miss. I be lost."

"You fool. My aunt is ill and she is getting worse by the moment. We really must stop very soon. I had hoped to be in Cornwall before dark and now it seems unlikely. Take us to the nearest town and ask for directions to a hotel – and hurry."

The driver looked suitably ashamed and crawled back onto his box. Luella shut the carriage door forcefully and sat down with a noisy exhalation of breath.

"The man is an idiot," she muttered, as her aunt sat huddled under a blanket. "I have asked him to stop at the next town so that we might find somewhere to stay. Can you last that long?"

"I shall try," replied her aunt wearily. "I don't think we can make it to Cornwall tonight, however."

"No, you are right," answered Luella, watching the sun sink in the sky.

The carriage rattled on down the country road and Luella felt tense as she watched her aunt become paler and paler.

After having searched Great Torrington for a hotel only to find nothing suitable, they were just going over a rather rickety wooden bridge when the carriage wheel hit a pothole and was thrown up in the air.

Although it landed safely without overturning, Aunt Edith let out a cry and fainted onto the floor of the carriage.

"Aunt! Aunt!" cried Luella, rushing to pick her up. But the Countess was too heavy for her and she had to call to the driver for help.

"I be sorry, miss. Couldn't help the hole," he said shame-faced as they hauled the Countess back into her seat.

"Just get us to a hotel quickly! Where are we?"

"I'll stop at the next inn and ask, miss."

The next inn, however, was not for miles and by now, it was almost dark.

The carriage passed a sign saying '*Bideford one mile*' and Luella instructed the driver to head in that direction.

But in Bideford, everywhere was as dead as a grave. They crossed a bridge over a wide river and then Luella saw it.

High on the hill overlooking the riverbank was a large and elegant house.

'It could be a hotel or it could be a private house,' she conjectured. 'In any case, it must belong to someone of importance so I shall have to throw myself on their mercy. Perhaps they will be able to direct us to a suitable place to stay. Aunt Edith cannot continue for much longer in this carriage without collapsing.'

She ordered the driver to proceed through the iron gates and up the winding drive towards the house.

By now the sky overhead was dark and the wind rustled through the trees, making them appear forbidding and gloomy.

'I hope they are not, as some country folk are, suspicious of strangers or worse, half mad,' Luella murmured to herself.

As they drew nearer, she could see that the house was in a rundown state and her heart sank. She noted the missing windowpanes and the rusting ironwork.

The driver opened the carriage door and Luella stepped down, her heart racing.

"Wait here," she ordered firmly, as she walked towards the oak front door.

'Well,' she said to herself. 'I must be brave and enquire – there is no other nearby house and it does look as if someone is at home. There is a candle burning in that downstairs window.'

Lifting up the huge knocker, she let it fall, then took two steps back and waited as the hollow sound reverberated through the depths of the shabby building.

CHAPTER FOUR

Inside Torr House Cork wearily walked towards the front door.

All afternoon the steady stream of curious visitors to Torr House had not ceased. Everyone, it seemed, wanted to meet the new owner, who, gossip said, was the grandson of the old Marquis who used to visit his 'Frenchwoman' there.

And every other person came to offer their services.

"We've 'eard that the Frenchwoman's house is to be sold," they started.

"No, it is not. His Lordship intends to live in it."

"Is he really knocking it down? T'would be a shame if he were," said others.

Cork fervently hoped that this latest caller would not demand to see inside the house or to 'have a word' with the Viscount, for he had given strict instructions that he was not to be disturbed in the library where he was working.

Never had Cork seen such dedication.

"If it were up to his Lordship, the whole place would be rebuilt by the end of the week," he jokingly told his wife.

Cork opened the heavy door and was surprised to find a very attractive young lady. By her clothes he judged that she was not a local and viewed her with interest.

"Good afternoon, miss," he said politely.

"I am so sorry to trouble you," began Luella. "But my aunt, the Countess of Ridgeway, is ill and we cannot find a hotel and our coachman is lost. I wondered if you might be able to direct us?"

Cork cast a glance towards the carriage.

Although the young lady on the doorstep seemed genteel enough, he noted that she and her aunt were travelling in a hired coach. He hesitated as he tried to think of somewhere they could stay.

He knew there was a large cattle market and fair on the next day that people from miles around would visit. Inevitably all the hotels would be full.

"Would you wait here awhile, Miss – ?"

"Ridgeway. Luella Ridgeway," answered Luella anxiously.

As Cork went off to consult his wife, the Viscount emerged from the library.

"Who is that at the door?" he asked looking extremely tired. He hoped that it was not another person claiming to be a close friend of his grandfather's whom he would have to ask Cork to turn away.

"A young lady, my Lord. She is travelling with her sick aunt and they are lost. The aunt is the Countess of Ridgeway, as the young lady claims and they are travelling in a common hired carriage."

Intrigued the Viscount moved up the hall and the sight he glimpsed through the open door made his heart skip a beat.

There on his doorstep was the most beautiful woman he had ever seen.

Her fair hair framed her face like wispy clouds while her pale-blue eyes darted around nervously. Her whole demeanour was one of someone in need of rescuing and it appealed to his masculine instincts to come to her aid.

"Show her in, Cork."

"My Lord?"

"Don't stand there, man. Show her in."

Utterly shocked, Cork retraced his steps to the front door and threw it open.

"His Lordship has asked that you enter," he intoned with raised eyebrows.

"Thank you very much," sighed Luella, hoping that this nobleman was kind and that they would soon be on their way.

The hall somewhat surprised Luella. Although the house had undoubtedly once been grand, everywhere were signs of neglect.

'Yet, this man who approaches looks every inch the fine Lord,' she said to herself, as the Viscount came towards her with his hand outstretched.

"Miss Ridgeway? I am David Kennington. Welcome to my home. I hear you are lost and that your aunt is unwell."

"Yes, she is in the carriage outside. I was hoping to find a hotel where we might stay before continuing our journey. We were on our way to Bude in Cornwall and our fool of a driver took the wrong turn and we ended up on the Bideford road. We have been travelling in Europe and I am not familiar with this part of the country."

"They will not find anywhere tonight, my Lord," said Cork, who was standing nearby. "The cattle market and fair is on tomorrow."

"Then, you must stay here," exclaimed the Viscount. "Although I confess that the house is not as it should be. I only arrived here yesterday to find it in a state of disrepair."

"There is the blue room and the river room, my Lord.

They have been unaffected by the damp," suggested Cork suddenly. "Madame's visitors stayed there and they are most comfortable. Mrs. Cork and I made certain that they were ready to occupy as we did not know how many people to expect."

"Oh, I could not impose," cried Luella.

"Miss Ridgeway, I cannot have you wandering the roads of North Devon with an ill relative," replied the Viscount firmly. "Cork, have the Countess brought inside at once and take her to the blue room. Then send for the doctor."

"Yes, my Lord."

"Really, you must not go to any trouble."

"I would not hear of your travelling to the next town," the Viscount insisted, ushering Luella into the drawing room. "Now Cork will bring you some refreshments and we shall put your aunt to bed. One of the maids will sit with her until the doctor arrives. If you will excuse me, I must go and change as I have been working since early this morning and am not at my best."

With a short bow the Viscount left the room and Luella stared after him.

'What a fine-looking fellow,' she murmured as he closed the door.

Very soon, Mrs. Cork bustled into the room with another servant who carried a tray of tea and sandwiches.

"His Lordship will not be dining until half-past eight, miss, so he thought you might care for something light to eat after your journey."

She bent closer to Luella and whispered,

"And don't you worry. We've sent that rascal of a coachman packing. Your aunt is in bed now and a maid is looking after her. The doctor will be here soon and we will call you when he arrives."

"Thank you very much. You are all being *so* kind."

"We've always taken care of visitors at Torr House," said Mrs. Cork. "And I can see you are strangers here. Now eat your sandwiches and I'll come and fetch you when your room is ready."

'Who is this Viscount?' she asked herself. 'And what is he doing in this shabby house?'

She rose and examined an oil painting on the wall of a lady in a ball gown. Judging by her apparel, Luella thought that it had been painted some twenty or thirty years earlier.

"How beautiful she is," she declared. "Such wondrous eyes!"

"Yes, she is rather lovely, isn't she?" came a voice from behind her. "She was French, you know."

She turned around to see the Viscount standing in the doorway.

He had changed and was wearing a well-cut shirt and waistcoat over smart trousers. His shirt was open at the neck and his dark hair fell forward on one side in a highly attractive manner. His brown eyes were lively under black eyebrows.

"Is she a relative?" asked Luella a little self-consciously.

"No, she was – a family friend. I see that Mrs. Cork has attended to you?"

"Yes, thank you. It is most kind of you."

"Think nothing of it, Miss Ridgeway. I am a stranger myself to these parts and would hope that were I in the same position, someone would do likewise for me."

"What brings you to Bideford, if I may ask?" she said, fluttering her eyelashes as she looked up at him.

The Viscount found himself compelled to gaze into her blue eyes as they met his.

"My grandfather left me this house when he died recently. I hankered after a change in scenery as I had tired of London and this house offered me a unique opportunity. I am an architect, you see – or at least, I trained as such."

"So you have great plans for this house?" asked Luella sitting down again.

The Viscount noticed the shy way she regarded him. She tilted her head downwards and cast her eyes upwards in a manner that was rather beguiling. Lost in the moment he hesitated before replying.

"Yes, I wish to remodel the existing house and add to it. It would be a pity to tear down a fine house such as this and start again and I often find myself outraged at what has been done to many fine old houses in the name of progress and modernity."

"Well spoken," she agreed. "I am much of the same opinion. In France they do not tear down an old house because it is out of fashion. They respect the past."

"So, what finds *you* in the West Country?" he enquired, leaning on the mantelpiece and crossing one leg over the other.

Luella hesitated and then took a deep breath.

"I hope you will not think ill of me when I tell you – " she sighed, taking out a handkerchief and wrapping it around her delicate hands.

"You are not an infamous woman on the run from the Police, I hope!"

"No," answered Luella. "But I am fleeing from someone. An unwanted and persistent admirer."

"I would have thought that he would not be alone," muttered the Viscount, entranced by the vision of loveliness in front of him. "You must have many men at your feet."

"This man has decided that he is going to marry me –

he is obsessed!" she said looking down at her fingers. "We fled France when he became threatening and were to take refuge in Cornwall before returning to my aunt's house in Scotland. We both fell ill on the crossing and although I have recovered, she has not. I hope you will not think again about giving us refuge. You may not wish to harbour two fugitives!"

But the Viscount had already fallen under her spell.

It had been a very long time since he had felt so taken with a woman. His hardened heart had neither sought love nor missed it in his life, yet now he found himself swamped with myriad emotions.

Luella stared at him as she awaited his reply, but the Viscount found himself strangely hesitant. At last, he said,

"You have done nothing wrong. This man must have been very persistent to have followed you through Europe. Is it love that propels him so?"

"Not entirely. My aunt is a very rich and powerful woman with vast estates in Scotland. I am her only heir as the rest of the family have died. Frank Connolly, for that is the man's name, desires riches and power for himself. I am just another possession to be added into the bargain."

A fierce protectiveness sprang up in the Viscount's bosom. He felt outraged that this fortune hunter had so relentlessly pursued the lovely young lady who sat trembling in the chair in front of him. And because of him, her aunt was now ill.

He listened as Luella recounted the tale of Frank Connolly's reign of terror.

"Aunt Edith thought that if we travelled West, instead of going straight to London, we would shake him off. I was certain that he will be in pursuit of us."

"While you are under my roof, you must not fear for

your safety," the Viscount assured her with a tremor in his voice.

He rose from his chair and rang the bell.

"Dinner will be at half-past eight and I hope you will do me the honour of joining me?"

"I would be delighted," accepted Luella puzzled at his sudden change of mood.

As the Viscount left, Cork entered the room and informed Luella that the doctor was upstairs with the Countess. She stood up and followed him.

Meanwhile the Viscount was in the library gazing out of the window deep in thought.

His mind whirled and he found he could not concentrate, such was the effect that his beautiful visitor had on him.

'It is as if this house is casting a spell,' he told himself, as he looked out of the window at the wilderness of his garden.

The clock in the hall chimed six-thirty and the Viscount found himself wishing the hours away until dinner. He tried to sit down at his desk and do some more work, but his mind persisted in dwelling on the beautiful Luella Ridgeway.

'It's this place that is unnerving me so,' he decided picking up his instruments. 'And the ghost of Madame Le Fevre!'

*

The doctor was most adamant.

"She must rest for at least a week," he said as he packed up his bag. "She must drink lots of fluids and eat light and nourishing meals."

"But we cannot impose upon the Viscount's hospitality

for that long," replied Luella. "He has already been too kind."

"Move her at your own peril," counselled the doctor. "I cannot be held answerable if she resumes her travels earlier than I have stated."

The Countess was propped up in bed and being tended to by Maisie, who was making a great deal of fuss of her ensuring that she had everything she needed.

"We'll soon have you better, my Lady," she cooed. "But you must stay where you are."

Luella approached the bed and sank down on the edge of it. Her aunt, although still ghastly white, did look a little more comfortable.

"How are you feeling, Aunt Edith?"

"I am so grateful to the Viscount for taking us in," she whispered. "You must thank him for me."

"I have already done so."

"He is from London, is he not? Is he one of the Mayfair Kenningtons?"

"I have not asked, but it is obvious that he is not born locally."

"We are highly fortunate to have landed on his doorstep," added Aunt Edith. "Frank Connolly will never find us here!"

"I do hope not. I feel safe under the Viscount's roof – no matter how shabby it might be."

Luella sat with her aunt until it was time for dinner.

*

Meanwhile downstairs in the dining room, the Viscount was nervously pacing the room awaiting the arrival of Luella.

Cork noticed that his new Master appeared jittery, but

attributed it to the fact that he was anxious about entertaining visitors so soon after his arrival.

Of course, he was quite accustomed to serving strange faces as Madame Le Fevre had often taken in lost travellers. It was the position of the house, standing so prominently on the slopes above the River Torridge that attracted them to the door.

"Cork, would you see if Miss Ridgeway is coming?" asked the Viscount.

Almost as soon as the words had left his mouth, Luella appeared in the doorway wearing a beautiful blue silk dress that had obviously come from Paris.

The Viscount caught his breath as he gazed at her coming towards him, a shy smile playing about her lips.

"You are looking most charming this evening," declared the Viscount, as he took her hand and kissed it. Her soft skin smelled of lemon verbena that made him think of a fresh summer's day.

Luella smiled and blushed.

She did not feel in any way threatened by the Viscount for he was as different from Frank Connolly as was humanly possible. For a start, the Viscount was far nobler than Connolly, himself only the youngest son of a minor Irish Lord.

And Luella sensed at once that he subscribed to the highest moral values and would never seek to press his attentions on her.

"How is the Countess?" he asked, indicating to Cork to pour the wine.

"She is very comfortable, thanks to your wonderful maid."

"Yes, Maisie is a good and loyal servant. I am most fortunate that all my staff are excellent."

Cork brought the first course and they both ate in silence.

'Why am I being so awkward around her?' thought the Viscount, as he finished his dish. 'There is something about her that makes me behave like a stumbling fool.'

As the meal progressed, Luella seemed to relax and began to ask him questions.

"Do your family mind you being so far away from London?"

"I am not currently on speaking terms with my father," admitted the Viscount. "And Mama died a few years ago. I do miss Grandmama, but as she now lives in my father's house, we have limited contact."

"That is a pity," replied Luella, her large blue eyes full of compassion. "From what you say, you are the only son, I assume?"

"Yes, I have no brothers or sisters."

"I am in the same position and both my parents died in a terrible train crash in Scotland some years ago. I went to live with my uncle's wife, the Countess, and, when her husband died, she took to travelling around Europe, so I went with her."

"Oh, I am sorry," murmured the Viscount, as every inch of him longed to reach across the dining table and take her hand. "She is all you have in the world?"

"Yes, which is why I was so distraught when she collapsed in the carriage. I do not know what I should do if she were to – "

Her voice trailed off and the Viscount found his heart surging out to her.

She awakened so many unfamiliar emotions in him that his first instinct was to distance himself from her.

Yet, as she sat there before him, her soft hair curling

around her face and her small but expressive hands fluttering, he was as one hypnotised.

*

Later in the darkness of his cavernous and chilly room, the Viscount swore he could still smell the scent of verbena clinging to the air.

Sleep did not come easily that night.

Although exhausted, he felt as if he was intoxicated – such was the effect Luella Ridgeway had exerted upon him.

When Hoskin awaked him the next morning, he grasped the proffered cup of tea and drained it eagerly before requesting another.

He was impatient to see Luella again.

"Is Miss Ridgeway up yet?" he asked as innocently as he could.

"I believe that she is with her aunt at the moment, my Lord. Do you wish to see her?"

"No, I shall see her soon enough at breakfast."

He had already decided to invite her to go out riding with him that morning. The day held the promise of being warm and fine.

As Hoskin finished dressing him, he practised in his head what he would say to her. His heart was racing as he entered the dining room and Luella was already seated.

"Good morning, I trust you slept well and that the room was to your liking?" he said with a slight bow.

"Very well, thank you. It was a relief to be in a proper bed again after our endless travels."

"I intend to replace all the furniture once work on the house has been completed," the Viscount told her. "I will keep some of the paintings, naturally, as they are both attractive and valuable, but the rest will be sold or given away."

"You must show me your designs," suggested Luella raising her cup to her rosy lips. "I should very much like to see them."

Emboldened the Viscount seized his opportunity.

"Perhaps you would care to come for a ride around the estate this morning with me? I confess that I have scarcely had a chance to view it properly myself and would welcome the company. You do ride, I assume?"

"Oh, yes," nodded Luella, enthusiastically. Her blue eyes lit up and became at once more animated as her mouth curved into a smile. "I love to ride but have not had much opportunity over the past year. In Scotland we have a fine stable of horses that I miss a great deal."

"Shall we meet outside in say an hour?" asked the Viscount. "I am afraid I do not have any suitable clothing to offer you."

"I have something that will do, although, I would need to borrow a crop."

"Cork will see to it. Cork!"

The butler spun round as he stood by the buffet stacking the empty dishes.

"There is an old riding outfit of Madame's in a wardrobe upstairs, if Miss Ridgeway would care to try it. I believe there is a crop and gloves as well."

"Excellent. Perhaps you would have Maisie go and fetch them at once."

Cork bowed and left the room.

Luella arose from the table and promised to meet the Viscount later.

At half-past ten sharp, the Viscount hurried down the stairs to meet her. Luella was already outside enjoying the sunshine.

"It's a beautiful day. What a pity Aunt Edith cannot

join us as she loves to ride."

"I have had to ask Cork how to get to the stables," said the Viscount, as they walked together around the outside of the house. "It is all still very new to me."

"I am very eager to see your designs," commented Luella. "Will you keep the outbuildings as they are now?"

"As I have yet to see them, I could not say and then, there is the problem of the gardens. Although I am perfectly capable of redesigning bricks and mortar – it is a different matter when it comes to flowers and foliage."

"I may be able to help you," said Luella with an enigmatic smile. "You must show the gardens to me after our ride."

The stables were far better than the Viscount had expected. There was a groom and a stable boy in attendance much to his surprise.

There were half a dozen or more horses and some pushed their heads out of their stall doors when they heard Joshua, the groom, approaching.

"I've selected Bonaparte, a sturdy black stallion for you, my Lord," said Joshua. "And for miss 'ere, there is Delphine, a dapple-grey mare. Don't be fooled by her pretty looks, miss, she's a sly one with a great turn of speed."

"Then, she shall suit me very well," exclaimed Luella flushed with excitement.

She followed Joshua to Delphine's stall and immediately took a liking to the spirited mare.

"We shall have a fine time together, Delphine," she said, as she stroked the mare's soft nose.

She tucked the crop that had once belonged to Madame Le Fevre under her arm and waited for Joshua to bring Delphine out of the stall. She was wearing the blue riding skirt and gloves that Maisie had found in the wardrobe.

The Viscount stood behind her and watched as Joshua pulled out the box for her to stand on to mount Delphine.

The sun glistened on her pale hair and the riding habit she wore suited her. He admired the way she mounted the mare so nimbly and her ease with a strange horse.

As soon as Bonaparte was ready, he hauled himself into the saddle and they trotted off away from the house.

The Viscount produced a rough map of the area covered by the estate and suggested they head for the far boundary and then traverse along the river before returning to the front of the house.

Luella surprised him by overtaking him almost as soon as they reached open countryside. Delphine, it appeared, did not need much persuasion to stretch her legs into a gallop.

Catching up with her by a small coppice, the Viscount complimented her on her prowess.

"I was put on a horse as soon as I could walk," she answered. "Papa was the finest horseman in Scotland and insisted that I be given the opportunity to follow in his footsteps, even though I was only a girl!"

"It was much the same with me," admitted the Viscount. "Father had an estate and house in Hertfordshire and we spent many summers there. Cork tells me that there is fine sport to be had on Exmoor and that people come from miles around to join the hunt."

"I do not care for riding to hounds. I find it tedious and pointless."

"I must attempt to show you the error of your ways," remarked the Viscount with a smile. "I shall ask Cork if the hunt meets before you return to Scotland."

Luella did not reply. She simply smiled and spurred Delphine into action and the Viscount was soon in pursuit.

After a few hours, he became quite fatigued and

signalled to Luella that they should return to the stables.

"A pity," she called, as they galloped back towards the house. "I feel as if I could ride all day on Delphine – she is a magnificent animal!"

"Joshua knew what he was doing when he chose her for you."

On their way back to the house, having returned the horses to Joshua, they wandered through the neglected gardens.

"What a shame," cried Luella, fondling an overgrown rose bush that was heavy with suckers and dead heads. "This is a very lovely rose with a wonderful perfume – *rosa damascena.* Whoever planted it here, knew it was the perfect spot for it. And look, this clematis has not been pruned for years and has become woody."

"You seem to know a great deal about gardening," commented the Viscount appreciatively.

"It's one of my passions in life," sighed Luella, as she inspected a drooping fuchsia bush. "In Scotland, I designed many of my neighbours' gardens."

She stopped for a moment and appeared to have an idea.

"I could do it for you!"

"The garden? I could not ask you – "

"It would be a wonderful way to repay your kindness," she insisted. "If you would allow me, I could sketch a plan for planting and add some suggestions for features – it would be great fun to work on such lovely surroundings. And so different from anything in Scotland."

The Viscount regarded her intently.

Her whole face was shining with enthusiasm as she flitted from bed to bed, examining what still lived and what had died.

"Please," she said pleadingly. "It would be such a pleasure to use my brain again after my year of idle self-indulgence."

"Well, if it would not be too much trouble," he began. "As I have said, I am no expert when it comes to horticulture."

"Then I shall start at once," replied Luella twirling around in delight. "But I shall need some help in the form of gardeners. Do you have any on your staff?"

"No, but if you would care to word an advertisement for me, Cork can place it in the local newspaper."

Luella ran towards him and much to his delight and astonishment put her arm through his.

"Good. It is all settled. Let us return to the house so that I can tell Aunt Edith at once."

Her blue eyes sparkled most attractively as she led him up the path to the rear of the house.

"I will make this garden something that everyone will talk about and praise to the skies," she asserted. "People will flock for miles around to view it and it will make your house all the more impressive."

With a skip, she ran across the hall, leaving the Viscount to gaze after her in admiration.

'Miss Ridgeway, you are full of surprises,' he mumbled, as he watched her mount the stairs, singing to herself.

As she did so, she stopped to cast a cheery smile towards the Viscount.

The moment their eyes met, something passed between them that made his heart leap.

Overcome with shyness, Luella blushed and tried to still her own beating heart.

*

In the bar of the *Grand Hotel* in Dover, Frank Connolly was in a foul mood.

Having spent the previous few days on trains and then a choppy crossing from Calais, he was infuriated to find that the trail had gone cold.

When he had finally exerted sufficient pressure upon the night porter at the hotel to tell him where the Countess and Luella had disappeared to, he had been so angry that he had slammed his whisky glass down so hard on the bar that it had shattered into a thousand pieces.

'She thinks that she can escape from me. Well, I will show her!' he had snarled.

At once he had packed his bags and taken a carriage to the station and from there, had caught the boat-train to Calais.

And now, he was standing in the lobby of the *Grand Hotel*, after searching almost every large establishment in town. But his enquiries about his 'sister-in-law and her aunt,' had fallen on fallow ground. No one had seen any such twosome.

At last, tired and hungry, he was forced to admit temporary defeat. He requested a room at the hotel and was waiting with his bags for the porter.

'She must be somewhere,' he said to himself. 'They will have gone straight to London. That is it.'

With each passing moment he was becoming more and more resolute.

'If Luella thinks she has got rid of me, she is very much mistaken,' he muttered, as he entered his room. He handed the porter a coin and slammed the door.

'If I have to hunt her down like a dog, I will,' he resolved. 'I will leave no stone unturned until she is mine!'

CHAPTER FIVE

Although the Viscount enjoyed entertaining guests, they also provided something of an unwelcome distraction to the task he had charged himself with.

He still arose early the next day and was at his new desk in the library by half-past six, but he found himself constantly listening out for signs that Luella was up and about.

When Cork asked him if he would care to take his breakfast as he worked, the Viscount found himself almost snapping at him.

"Certainly not. I shall eat in the dining room with our guest."

Later, as he sat and waited for Luella to appear, he became anxious and impatient.

Cork set some kidneys and bacon before him, but they remained untouched. He could not think of eating. He had too much on his mind.

"I do hope you have not waited for me," called Luella, in her soft voice, as she entered the dining room.

She was wearing a pale-blue dress that brought out the colour of her eyes.

He felt his heart race as she smiled at him and took her place at the table.

"Is your aunt better this morning?"

"Yes, much, thank you. I do believe the colour is returning to her cheeks. Mrs. Cork's nourishing food is doing her the world of good."

"I am very glad," replied the Viscount, toying with his breakfast. "I, myself, have always set great store by the health-giving properties of the countryside."

There was a momentary silence while Cork waited on Luella. Then she pulled out a piece of paper from her waistband and spread it out on the table.

"I have taken the liberty of sketching some rudimentary designs for the landscaping of the garden," she started proudly. "Would you care to see them?"

"Of course," agreed the Viscount taking the paper from her.

"I thought that the garden should be arranged in five terraces, seeing that it slopes upwards," she explained. "Any large bushes or shrubs should be planted at the perimeters, while the main planting should be in the centre of each area.

"Might I suggest a kitchen garden in this space as indicated," she waved her hand at the paper. "And each area will be linked with a series of arches and arbours."

"I am afraid you have lost me already. I know very little about technicalities, as I explained. You have me at your mercy."

As these last few words fell from his lips, he gazed at her underneath his intense black eyebrows and fancied that she blushed slightly. She had caught his meaning only too clearly.

Luella recovered herself and continued,

"Then there is the question of the gardeners. You will need full-time gardeners for gardens this size – might I offer to help you with that as well? I am well-versed in the instruction and management of such staff and would be only too happy to word and place an advertisement in your local newspaper."

"I thought you said that Cork could do it?"

"I rather fancy a trip into Bideford today," she said smiling. "It would be a pity to remain here until my aunt is better without a visit. I hear there is a pannier market on top of the hill."

"Cork will advise you. I have been here only a day longer than you and know very little of Bideford."

"Then, I shall ask Cork – it was just that Mrs. Cork mentioned I should see it."

"You must take Bennett in that case. He will drive you in my motor car."

"You have a *motor car*?" she asked eyes sparkling with excitement. "Although we saw them on the Continent, I have yet to experience one for myself."

"It is settled then. Bennett will take you whenever you wish. Cork, will you send word to him that Miss Ridgeway will require his services this morning?"

"Yes, my Lord."

They chatted pleasantly until Cork returned and informed them that Bennett was outside, whenever Miss Ridgeway was ready to leave. Luella excused herself from the table excitedly.

"Thank you so much," she cried. "This is such a treat. Aunt Edith will be very annoyed to have missed the opportunity."

"I am certain that there will be time for her to go for a drive when she is better. When is the doctor coming again?"

"Maisie said that he will be visiting again this afternoon, so I shall speak with him then. You will understand that we cannot linger here indefinitely – "

"You are still concerned that this Frank man will find you here?" asked the Viscount. "I can assure you, he will not. He would have to be a great clairvoyant, like Madame Blavatsky herself, to divine where you both are."

Luella hesitated in the doorway, her bottom lip trembling and giving her, he thought, a rather fragile air.

He longed to protect her and if he could root out this man and expunge him from the country – and from Luella's life – he would do so gladly and with his bare hands if necessary.

'Yes, I am just being foolish,' murmured Luella.

Maisie brought her hat and white cotton gloves. As the day was warm and fine, she had not thought it necessary to bring her a coat.

Luella sought out the oak mirror that hung at the far end of the hall and used it to arrange her hat to best effect.

"You will need more than hatpins to keep your hat on," teased the Viscount, as he watched her every move entranced. "I have seen other ladies secure theirs with a scarf. Do you have one?"

Luella thought for a moment and then dispatched Maisie back upstairs to retrieve a suitable item from the chest of drawers.

While she waited, she peeped out of the front door to where Bennett stood, looking very smart in his chauffeur's uniform, next to the Daimler.

"Will he drive very fast?" she asked.

"That is up to you," laughed the Viscount. "Bennett used to drive for an old Duke, who used to entreat him to go faster all the time. You will be in a safe pair of hands. Bennett is very experienced considering that this is a new-fangled invention."

Five minutes later, Luella was flushed with excitement

as she sat in the passenger seat alongside Bennett. Just as they were leaving, he tooted the horn for good measure and made her jump.

The Viscount felt inexplicably miserable as he watched the motor car disappear down the winding track to the main road. He wished he could have accompanied her into the town. How it would have delighted him to parade the streets of Bideford with Luella on his arm.

*

Luella found Bideford to be a charming town.

But she quickly discovered that she would have to go to Barnstaple if she wished to place an advertisement in the local paper. However, Bennett said he would be delighted to take her.

She bought flowers in Barnstaple for her aunt before proceeding to the offices of the *North Devon Journal* where she placed her advertisement.

"There!" she announced triumphantly. "It is all done and I have requested interested candidates to present themselves at Torr House on Friday."

"We should be heading for home now, Miss Ridgeway," Bennett suggested. "I believe I glimpsed a garage on our way into town and I must fill up the petrol tank."

By the time that they arrived back at Torr House, the Viscount was almost beside himself with worry.

When Luella did not appear for luncheon, he began to fret even though he knew it was impossible for Frank Connolly to be lurking in Bideford waiting to capture her.

When the Daimler eventually pulled up outside Torr House, the Viscount had to force himself not to run outside in a mixture of panic and relief.

"Where on earth have you been?" he asked, as Luella,

her face full of pleasure, was helped from the motor car by Bennett.

"I am so sorry, Lord Kennington," she said breezily, "but we had to drive to Barnstaple to place the advertisement. I have had such a wonderful afternoon. The countryside here is magnificent – even to the point of rivalling that of my homeland."

"That is praise, indeed, but come, you must be famished. Shall I have Cork bring you something to eat?"

"I am fine, thank you. I found a hotel in Barnstaple with a nice restaurant. Bennett was thrilled because he met another chauffeur and they had a jolly time discussing the combustion engine."

The Viscount laughed.

He loved the way that Luella found even the slightest thing amusing and that she never seemed to be depressed, even though she was so far from home.

"But now I should like to go and see Aunt Edith and take her these flowers I have bought for her. Cork, I assume the doctor has been to see her?"

"He has, Miss Ridgeway."

She ran swiftly up the stairs and along the landing to the blue room and was thrilled to see her out of bed and sitting in an armchair near the window.

"Aunt Edith. You are up," she cried rushing over to kiss her.

"Yes, I was feeling a little better. I must say, the local doctor here is as fine as anyone would find in Harley Street. He has worked miracles. He says I should be fit to travel by early next week. We can be on our way."

The Countess thought she glimpsed something like disappointment flash over Luella's lovely face before she recovered herself.

"So, that would explain why you are in such good

spirits," she exclaimed, turning away so her aunt could not see her expression. "As for myself, I have been so busy I have not had time to worry about Frank Connolly. Is that not wonderful?"

The Countess smiled and took her niece's hand, turning her back to face her.

"I have not seen you so animated for a very long time. The Devon air must suit you. Or perhaps it is a certain Viscount who has put a spring in your step?"

Luella coloured and withdrew her hand. She lowered her blue eyes and passed a hand across her burning cheeks.

"Oh, Aunt," she chided. "Your illness appears to have affected your sensibilities. You know that I could not possibly entertain the idea of romance and you know the reasons why."

"Really, child. I do not think that he is the kind of gentleman who would take issue with what is now well and truly in the past."

"He is a pleasant-enough fellow," interrupted Luella a little too swiftly. "And I like him well enough, but I can see that you are much better and at the mercy of fanciful notions. I shall have to ask Maisie to find you something to occupy yourself with."

"Stuff and nonsense! But Luella, if a chance for happiness presents itself, you should not dismiss it out of hand. Love is the most important thing in life."

"And I have plenty of it around me as long as I have you," replied Luella. "Any other love does not interest me in the least, and that is the way I intend it to be."

"He is very handsome, though – " interjected the Countess, then paused seeing Luella's cross expression.

'*Methinks the maiden doth protest too much,*' she sighed to herself, as her niece busied herself in the room, unnecessarily tidying what Maisie had already attended to earlier that morning.

*

The Countess did not wish to go down for dinner that evening, much to Luella's disappointment. After seeing her so sprightly that afternoon, she had hoped that she would join her and the Viscount in the dining room.

What her aunt had said to her was still playing on her mind as Maisie helped her to dress.

She entered the dining room to find the Viscount poring over a large sheet of paper on which there appeared to be some drawings.

"You have finished your plans for the house?" she asked as Cork pulled out a chair for her.

"Almost. I hope you do not mind, but I wish to solicit your opinion before I proceed. I was so impressed with your ideas for the gardens and it is obvious that you have a talent for design."

"Oh, but I am not an expert when it comes to architecture," she said shyly. "Plants and trees are my particular forte."

"Even so, I would be grateful if you would cast an eye over the plans."

He rose and moved towards Luella. As he approached her, the familiar scent of verbena wafted up, intoxicating him. He spread the paper in front of her and leaned over.

He could see the way loose hairs sprang up from her hairline, forming a corona about her head. Her skin was as white as a snowdrop and appeared velvety smooth.

As he explained his designs to her, he could hear her breathing and sense the rise and fall of her chest, which inordinately stirred him.

Coughing he moved away lest she sense his growing passion for her.

'I must not frighten her,' he told himself. 'She is nervous of men, that much is apparent and if I wish to set my cap at her, I should move cautiously.'

At Cork's insistence, he rolled up the paper and allowed him to serve dinner.

"They are, of course, far from complete," he admitted as he tucked the plans away under the table. "But it will have given you an idea of what I wish to achieve."

"It will be a wonderful building," she enthused, looking him straight in the eye. "I should not wonder if you will become famous because of it."

"That is what my grandfather would have wished," he said, feeling a pang of sadness. "He deeply desired that I should make a name for myself in the world of architecture."

"And, no doubt, you will."

There was a moment when they simply looked at each other. No words were spoken and the Viscount felt his heart contract.

'She feels it too,' he said to himself, as Luella blushed and looked down.

After dinner he asked if she would care to listen to music in the drawing room.

"I have brought my gramophone from London. And some recordings of my favourite classical pieces. Beethoven, Brahms, Chopin."

"I should like that very much," said Luella rising from her chair. "I admit I play the piano rather poorly, but I love music."

The Viscount offered her his arm and after a second's hesitancy, she took it.

Her bare arm felt warm against his jacket and the Viscount found himself wishing he could touch her soft skin.

Cork brought in coffee and wound up the machine

before placing a shellac disc on the turntable.

He brought the heavy arm across the gramophone and carefully set it down so that the needle touched the disc. After a good deal of hissing and a click, the sounds of a romantic piece by Chopin echoed around the room.

Luella soon found herself transported by the music.

"Oh, I did not want it to end," she sighed, as the needle hit the run-out groove of the disc and stuck there noisily.

"There is more," said the Viscount selecting a waltz by Strauss.

As soon as the music began, Luella could not keep her feet still. She traced the steps of the waltz where she sat and gazed into the distance, wishing that she was on a dance floor.

"You like to dance?" asked the Viscount seeing her feet moving.

"I adore to dance. There was not much opportunity to dance in Paris – "

Her voice trailed off and a far-away look came into her eyes. Seeing her recalling a distant memory, the Viscount leapt up.

"Then, dance with me now."

Luella regarded his handsome athletic figure and, judging that he would be fine partner, rose from her chair.

"Very well," she agreed in a low voice.

She cast her eyes downwards as he took her in his arms. The music was still playing as they began to slowly waltz around the drawing room.

All too soon the record coming to an end shattered the Viscount's reverie. He ran over to the gramophone, quickly wound it up and replaced the needle.

He took her once more into his arms and whisked her around the carpet. She was laughing and gay and the colour in her cheeks made her more beautiful than ever.

The Viscount's head whirled as they moved together and this time, as the music stopped, their faces were just inches apart.

Without thinking, he leaned forward and kissed her soft mouth – just for a second. It was a gentle kiss, like rain falling upon a petal.

His heart soared up to Heaven as for a second Luella returned the kiss, but then pulled away.

"*David*," she breathed her voice hoarse with bewilderment.

"Oh, I am sorry. I was so lost in the moment that I forgot myself. Luella, you are so very beautiful and you must know how I – "

"Hush," she said putting her fingers across his strong mouth. "It is not that I find you repellent, it is just that I don't only have myself and my feelings to take into consideration. There is Aunt Edith."

"Yes, of course. I apologise."

"It is not that I don't like you, David, but I am not as quick to make up my mind as you are. We should proceed very carefully."

"Naturally. Whatever you wish," he responded withdrawing from her.

"I hope you understand. I must take care of Aunt Edith as I am all she has."

"Yes, yes, you are right."

The Viscount moved towards the gramophone and took off the disc.

"I am actually rather tired all of a sudden," he said. "Would you excuse me? I think I shall retire for the evening."

It was now Luella's turn to feel a little wrong-footed,

but she was so torn with conflicting emotions that she simply nodded.

"Goodnight, Luella, and thank you for a very special evening."

He bowed and left the room leaving Luella alone and confused.

'Damn my stupid impulsiveness,' he hissed to himself, as he mounted the stairs two at a time. 'I have probably frightened her away now – and that is the last thing I would wish to happen.'

*

All too soon Friday dawned and the Viscount realised that Luella would soon be leaving Torr House.

He was surprised to see a queue of men outside the house by ten o'clock, all waiting to be interviewed for the post of gardener.

'She is a marvel,' he thought, as Cork led the parade of candidates to the kitchen, where Luella was ready and waiting for them.

Two hours later, Luella emerged from below stairs looking delighted.

"Two highly experienced gardeners will start at once," she announced, throwing herself down onto a Chippendale chair in the library. "Cork is showing them the grounds and then will fetch me to instruct them where to begin."

"Excellent," acknowledged the Viscount, looking up from his drawing board.

He had barely sketched two lines since breakfast, instead preferring to go over and over in his mind the events of the previous evening.

"They will live out until the house is finished," continued Luella. "How are your plans for the house coming along?"

The Viscount sighed and put down his pencil.

"Slowly. It is a difficult task and I have encountered a problem with where to site the orangery I had planned."

"Does it have to be attached to the house?"

"Well, no – "

"Then, what about the wall at the side of the lower terrace? The one nearest the kitchen? Could not a structure be erected there?"

"Of course. Brilliant, simply brilliant!"

"You are not seeing the wood for the trees," suggested Luella impishly.

She got up and walked over to his drawing board and examined his drawings.

She stood so close to the Viscount that he was almost overcome with love for her.

"It will be a very fine house," she said appreciatively. "I do believe I would like to live in such a place."

Enraptured by her nearness the Viscount could not help himself.

"You could, Luella – *if you agreed to be my wife!*"

Almost as soon as the words had left his lips, he realised he had made a grave error in giving voice to his feelings.

Luella's expression changed from rapt interest to chilly distance, as she moved away from the drawing board and towards the door.

"I have just remembered, there is a letter I should write informing the servants at Aunt Edith's home to make ready for our return. Much as we have enjoyed your hospitality, we are eager to see our own beds again. Now, if you will excuse me – "

With a swishing of skirts, she left the room.

The Viscount thumped his fist down on his drawing board.

"Damn! Damn!" he cried. "Now, I have lost her. I should not have blurted out what I was thinking. I am such a *fool*."

*

He did not see Luella again until dinner that evening.

Even the arrival of a new telephone, an event that had caused much excitement with the servants, did not appear to interest her when he had tried to demonstrate it.

The Countess joined them, which served to make the atmosphere less strained.

Luella looked lovelier than ever and it hurt the Viscount to see her act in such a cool manner towards him.

"You really must come and stay with us in Perthshire," Aunt Edith was saying, enjoying Mrs. Cork's *minestrone* soup. "Braemore Castle, although ancient and a little draughty, is splendid in August. You could come in time for the grouse."

The Viscount cast a glance at Luella and saw a look of dismay cross her features, so he replied,

"Thank you, but I shall be occupied here with the renovations. I intend to have the builders begin work the moment I have finished the plans. In fact some will be arriving next week to knock down some old outbuildings and I have taken your suggestion of siting the orangery near the kitchen, Luella."

"My niece is a very clever young lady," observed the Countess. "If she was a man, she would be the most successful in whichever field she chose to specialise."

"Aunt, you are making me blush," exclaimed Luella, putting down her spoon. "Besides, Lord Kennington is a most brilliant architect – of that I have no doubt."

When she spoke about him, Luella did not look directly at him and it hurt that she referred to him so formally. He loved to hear his name on her lips.

"I shall be sorry to leave on Monday," continued the Countess. "We shall go to London for a week – the coast should be clear and, no doubt, Frank Connolly will have given up chasing around trying to find us."

"You are quite welcome to stay as long as you like," offered the Viscount.

"Thank you, but we wish to return home after shopping in London. We have been away for long enough," jumped in Luella.

Her swift retort stung the Viscount and he resolved to speak with her alone as soon as he could.

'She is obviously deeply offended by my sudden proposal,' he thought, 'and I do not wish her to feel as if I am another troublesome pest in her life.'

As they retired to the drawing room the Viscount took Luella to one side.

"Luella, I fear I have upset you by proposing," he said, as the Countess tactfully left them alone.

She flushed deep scarlet.

"You have not," she replied awkwardly. "I confess I was taken aback by you, but I do not find the idea out of the question. Just not yet awhile, that is all – "

The Viscount took her hand in his, ever so gently, and looked into her eyes.

"Might I hope?"

"Let me think on what you have said, David, and I promise I will give you an answer after I have returned home. I will need to consult Aunt Edith."

"Of course," he answered eagerly.

"Now, we should join her as she will be wondering where we are."

Luella turned and left the dining room.

The Viscount paused for a moment and breathed deeply to calm himself.

'She has not said no,' he thought. *'There is hope yet.'*

Later, as they finished their coffee, the Viscount announced that, rather than stay in a hotel, he proposed they should use his house in South Audley Street.

"I shall telephone the servants and ask them to make the house ready for you," he said. "Bennett will take you to the station in Barnstaple. I would not hear otherwise so please do not protest."

"Thank you, it is most kind of you," said the Countess.

"You will not want for anything while you are under my roof."

The Viscount shot a look at Luella and a surge of love filled his heart.

'Please say *yes*,' he urged her silently, as she chatted gaily with her aunt. 'My life is utterly in your hands.'

*

It was with a heavy heart that the Viscount waved goodbye to the Countess and Luella the following Monday morning.

Almost as soon as they left, Torr House felt enormous and empty.

With a resigned sigh, he returned to his drawing board and worked as hard as he could. The builders were due later that week and there was no time to spare.

The Countess enjoyed her ride in the Daimler immensely and remarked to Luella that she might consider buying such a machine once they had returned to Scotland.

"Think of all the day trips we can make to the Highlands," she mused. "And I do not wish to sit and grow old without something to look forward to."

Luella laughed as the Countess sat beaming in the passenger seat.

They both felt incredibly sad to leave Torr House.

Luella found she had a lump in her throat as they reached the end of the drive, as she realised that she would not see the Viscount again for a long while.

*

And whilst they were boarding the train to Exeter and onwards to London, in a small Duke Street hotel, Frank Connolly was registering himself as a guest.

"How long will you be staying with us, Mr. Connolly?" asked the clerk.

"I don't know. Perhaps a week, perhaps longer."

"Very well, sir. Now, if you will follow the porter, he will see that you are settled into your room. I hope you have a pleasant stay."

Frank Connolly grunted with ill humour.

He had no intention of having a pleasant stay. He had one matter on his mind – and one only.

Once inside he dropped his bag to the floor and cast a perfunctory glance around the room. He then went straight out again.

It was a rainy day in London and for July a trifle chilly. Frank Connolly buttoned up his coat with its old-fashioned caped shoulders against the drizzle and bent his head low as he made his way to Marylebone High Street.

There in a quiet side street he entered an open doorway and ascended the grubby stairs.

Outside, the brass plaque read *Henry Jones, Private Detective*.

At the top of the stairs, he twisted the black doorknob and entered. A secretary asked his name and bade him sit down.

A few moments later, he was in Mr. Jones's office, showing him a photograph of Luella.

"I want you to find my – sister-in-law at all costs," he began and then adjusted his tone when he saw the look on Mr. Jones's face. "She disappeared months ago and has come into an inheritance that she knows nothing about and I have been charged to find her. My late brother would have wished it."

"It will not be cheap, Mr. Connolly," said Mr. Jones, taking the photograph and examining it. "But she is a fine-looking woman. Should not be too hard to track her down. A toff, you say?"

"I have reason to believe that she is travelling with the Countess of Ridgeway."

"Then, we shall find her, rest assured, Mr. Connolly. At this time of year the nobs desert London, so if she's here, I'll soon track her down."

"Spare no expense," said Frank Connolly, as he put on his hat and rose to leave. "She must be found at any cost."

As he descended the stairs, he felt a sense of growing satisfaction.

'She will not be able to hide for much longer and I have ascertained that they have yet to return to Scotland, so they can only be in London,' he murmured. 'If Jones is as good as his reputation states, then, Luella Ridgeway, wherever you are, I shall discover your whereabouts and claim you!'

Rubbing his hands together in glee he emerged onto the street with something approaching a smile on his face.

CHAPTER SIX

Luella and the Countess arrived at Paddington station late that night exhausted from their long and arduous journey.

They were surprised to find that the Viscount had arranged for them to be met by his large and gleaming phaeton.

"These cannot be the Viscount's footmen," whispered Luella, as she helped her aunt settle into the carriage. "Did he not say that only two servants remained in his London home? He must have hired them especially for the occasion."

"He is, indeed, a generous man," commented the Countess. "But that is hardly surprising considering he is a man in love – "

"*Aunt!*"

Luella blushed to the roots of her hair and cast her eyes downwards as Aunt Edith continued,

"But I am right, am I not? *He is in love with you.*"

Luella looked down at her gloves and bit her bottom lip.

"He has asked me to marry him."

"Then, why, my dear girl, did you not accept? I am assuming that you did not, otherwise he would have come to speak with me."

"I cannot and you know the reasons why."

"I know of *one* reason why you believe yourself not worthy of him and I hope the other was not me. I am perfectly capable of looking after myself and going back to Scotland on my own."

"Aunt, I would not hear of it. But you are right about the other reason."

"The shadow of Jean-Marie Bouillicault still casts a shadow over you even now, nearly a year later?"

The Countess shook her head and took Luella's hand in hers.

"Luella, dearest, it was not your fault what happened."

"But I was engaged to him after a whirlwind romance that would have caused a scandal as it was. And, worse still, I ran away with him only to find that he was already married to another! How foolish will David think me? In addition, he will view me as second-hand goods."

"Darling, everyone knows that your virtue was never compromised by him. I would vouch for your purity. Besides, no one in England has heard of him and you were not named in the French newspapers, so what is there to worry about?"

"I think he will no longer love me if he discovers the truth," she sighed.

"And do you love him?" asked her aunt. "I can see that something has been troubling you deeply and I have been wondering – "

"*Oh, yes*," replied Luella fervently. "It was only when we were on the train that I realised just how much. I did not expect it to be such a wrench to leave him. But, with each passing mile, I felt distressed to no longer be with him."

"Then, do not hesitate, darling, seize your chance of happiness."

"Excuse me, my Lady. We are here."

The carriage had come to a halt and the footman was on the pavement, holding open the door.

Luella looked up at the elegant house with its walls of red London brick and black-framed windows.

An electric light burned in the hall of number 23, South Audley Street and Luella could see a butler waiting for them.

"Welcome, Miss Ridgeway. My Lady. My name is Bellamy," he said bowing to them. "If you would come this way, you will be shown straight to your rooms."

Luella was delighted to find that she had been given a large room with a comfortable bathroom. She was so tired, she did not bother to unpack. Instead she undressed, put on her nightdress and went straight to bed.

'I wonder where Frank Connolly is?' she asked herself as she drifted off. 'But I feel so safe beneath the Viscount's roof, I really must stop worrying.'

*

At the same time in Torr House, Hoskin, found his Master pacing the bedroom when he entered with a glass of water.

"Will that be all, my Lord?"

"Thank you, yes."

Hoskin closed the door and left the Viscount alone with his thoughts. Taking his candle to the mirror, he held up the long blonde hair that he had found on the back of the sofa and admired it as if it was a holy relic.

'Luella,' he muttered. 'I would have not believed how much I could miss you already.'

*

The next few days were highly enjoyable for Luella and the Countess.

The Viscount's carriage was totally at their disposal and they took a great many trips in it – Bond Street, Knightsbridge, Kew Gardens and the museums at South Kensington, to name but a few.

At first, they did not pay any heed to the man in the bowler hat and checked overcoat, who lingered in the shadows wherever they went.

He watched as they emerged from a fashionable Bond Street couturier and noted down the time, and he stood silently in a doorway as they left Harrods, burdened down with packages.

He wrote down everything he saw until he was satisfied that he had garnered enough information to report back to his client.

Mr. Jones sent a message to Frank Connolly's hotel and asked him to come to his office at once.

Barely two hours later, he was at the door, impatiently pacing around the waiting room.

"Mr. Jones will not be much longer," said the secretary, after he had demanded for the third time in fifteen minutes to see the detective.

At last the door opened and Mr. Jones's previous client emerged. Before he had put his hat on and left, Frank Connolly had barged his way into the inner office.

"You said you had something for me. Well, what is it?"

His watery eyes bulged and his ruddy face wore an air of expectation.

"There have been positive sightings of the ladies in question," Mr. Jones informed him. "Shopping at Harrods yesterday afternoon, for example."

"Do you expect me to lounge around Harrods all day on the off-chance of finding them? I need an address of where they are staying."

"Mr. Connolly, your, erhem, sister-in-law appears to be travelling around London in a rather fine and speedy carriage. I am afraid that I have not, as yet, been able to discover their exact location – "

"Well, get on to it, man! It is most urgent that I speak with Miss Ridgeway. You do not seem to understand."

Mr. Jones eyed the red-faced man who now leaned over the desk at him. He did not care for this client in the least and he was certain that the lady he was stalking was not his sister-in-law at all.

But it was not his business to ask questions when the client was paying so handsomely for his services.

Frank Connolly pulled a large denomination note out of his pocket and threw it on the desk in front of Mr. Jones.

"Is this enough? Find them before the end of the week and you shall receive another of these. Whatever it costs, I will pay. *But find her.*"

He spun on his heel and left the office. Mr. Jones let out a sigh of relief as he folded the note into four and tucked it into his wallet.

He had his suspicions who the expensive carriage belonged to, but first he wanted to be sure.

He waited for a while and then, picking up his bowler hat from the coat stand, he informed his secretary that he would be out for the rest of the day.

His destination was only a short walk to the other side of Oxford Street and he would have to hurry if he was to catch his prey returning from an afternoon out.

'These ladies are creatures of habit,' he murmured, as he walked quickly along James Street. 'They should be returning any time now.'

*

Luella and the Countess climbed down from their

carriage with a sense of exhaustion. They had visited all the most famous galleries in London and had taken tea at the Ritz.

Now with aching feet, they were looking forward to a quiet evening and one of Mrs. Bellamy's delicious meals.

As Luella helped her aunt down the carriage steps, she glanced across the road and noticed a man in a bowler hat hanging around near a tree.

"Do you know, Aunt Edith, I am certain we saw that man in Harrods yesterday afternoon, and he was in Hyde Park when we went for our walk the other morning. Do you recall how I remarked about him and joked that he was following us?"

Even though she attempted to make a joke of it, Luella was deathly pale. There was only one thought in her mind as to who might be responsible – and that was Frank Connolly.

The Countess stood on the pavement and put her lorgnette to her eye.

"Why, you are right, Luella, and I do believe he is up to no good."

Before Luella could stop her, the Countess was striding across the road waving her umbrella menacingly.

"You sir," she called. "Be off with you or I will call the Police. I have your description and do not think for a moment that I am a frail old woman who will not carry out her threat."

Mr. Jones quickly ran down the street. He knew a formidable woman when he saw one. The Countess followed him for a few yards before she judged that she had chased him away.

'No harm done,' he told himself, as he sped around the corner. 'That is the Countess of Ridgeway all right and they are staying at Lord Kennington's place, just as I suspected. Mr. Connolly will be pleased – very pleased indeed.'

The Countess was quite out of breath by the time she returned to the house. She had only given chase for a few yards, but had thoroughly enjoyed every moment.

Luella, however, was in the drawing room, sobbing her heart out.

"He has found us! *He has found us*!" she moaned, wringing her handkerchief. "That man is a private detective. I know it."

"He has been sent packing now," crowed the Countess proudly. "But I think we should curtail our stay in London and pack our boxes tonight. It is a pity, but Frank Connolly has ruined what was a very pleasant interlude."

"We cannot go to Scotland – it is the first place he will come looking for us."

"What do you suggest?"

"Can we not return to Torr House? You could telephone Lord Kennington and beg him to give us sanctuary once again."

The Countess thought for a moment and then, quietly asked Bellamy to put in a telephone call to Torr House.

"Please fetch me as soon as the exchange puts you through," she said, returning to the drawing room to comfort Luella as best she could.

Ten minutes later the telephone in the hall rang and Bellamy came in to inform them that their call had been connected.

"His Lordship is on the line, my Lady, and is waiting to speak with you."

The Countess quickly outlined their predicament to the Viscount.

"Frank Connolly has engaged a private detective to track us down and he has succeeded in locating us. Might we impose upon your hospitality again and return to Devon?

I do not think he could find us there."

"And Luella?"

"She is distraught as you can imagine."

"Oh, my poor darling!"

The Countess smiled to herself as she thought,

'I am right in thinking that the Viscount is deeply in love with Luella. He will *not* spurn her when she tells him her secret.'

"Lord Kennington, it is not safe for us to remain here."

"Then, you must make all haste back to Devon. Will you instruct Bellamy to have your things packed and the carriage made ready? He must also find out what time the next train leaves Paddington for Exeter and I will have Bennett pick you up. Just tell Bellamy to inform me of the time you expect your train to arrive."

"Thank you, Lord Kennington. You do not know how grateful we are to you."

"It will be a long journey, but there is not a moment to lose," replied the Viscount, anxiety creeping into his deep voice. "If Frank Connolly really has discovered where you are, he will be relentless. In the meantime tell the servants not to admit anyone to the house and any callers are to be told that you have left for Scotland. If needs be, we must send him on a wild goose chase."

The Countess replaced the telephone on the stand and returned to the drawing room where Luella sat still crying.

"It is all in order," she told her. "Bellamy is having our boxes packed and the carriage made ready. I suggest that we leave via the mews at the rear so that if, by any chance, the front of the house is being watched, we shall depart undetected."

"How can you be certain that he will not attempt to creep up on us there?"

"Luella, for all his airs, Frank Connolly is a rather stupid and unsophisticated individual. It should not be difficult to outwit him. Now, come, we must get ready and quickly."

But Luella, rather than flying upstairs, remained rooted to the spot.

"I – *cannot*."

"Luella, you must. We cannot remain here. If that man is employed by Frank Connolly, then he will have gone straight to inform him of our whereabouts. We must make haste."

Luella stared at her in utter misery. Her face was blotched and her eyes were red-rimmed from crying.

"I do not think I can face another flight from him. Perhaps it would be better if I simply succumbed and married him."

"Luella! You must not say such things!" cried her aunt, drawing herself up to her full height. "I will not hear of it. What the Viscount said to me just now on the telephone has left me in no doubt that he is deeply in love with you. Dearest, you have a chance for happiness – you must endure the present difficulties, I beg you."

Luella remained on the sofa, uncertain what to do. She knew she loved the Viscount, but Frank Connolly had all but beaten the fight out of her.

"I am so tired of fleeing from him," she murmured, shaking her head. "*So very tired.*"

"This will be your last flight, I promise you," coaxed Aunt Edith. "Now, come with me and wash your face. We shall stay upstairs if you feel safer, but I am certain that Bellamy will not let anyone past the front door."

Eventually Luella allowed herself to be led upstairs.

"We must take only the bare necessities with us," said

the Countess. "I will have Bellamy arrange for the remainder to be sent directly to Scotland. It might provide a useful decoy for us, if this detective sees our luggage being taken off to King's Cross and not Paddington."

Once she had been persuaded, it did not take Luella long to pack some things into a suitcase and wait for Bellamy to tell them it was time to leave.

"The driver is ready for you, my Lady."

Bellamy was a big burly man and as he stood in the doorway he seemed to fill it. The Countess reckoned that he would more than acquit himself favourably should Frank Connolly become physically violent.

"Thank you, Bellamy. I shall tell Lord Kennington how kind you have been."

"It is nothing, my Lady. You are guests in his Lordship's house and he would expect me to do nothing less than I have already done."

They were halfway down the back stairs when there came a terrible knocking on the front door. They froze in their steps as the noise echoed throughout the house.

Bellamy looked at the Countess whose face wore a grim expression. She knew the knocking could mean only one thing. Frank Connolly had found them.

"Quickly, my Lady. If we get down the stairs to the kitchen, I will go and open the front door. I shall enjoy sending this man packing."

Bellamy led them through the scullery and out into the yard. Luella could hear the horses snorting as soon as they were outside and they hurried towards the carriage.

"*Let me in, you bounder.*"

Frank Connolly's harsh voice was so loud that it could be heard in the mews at the rear of the house.

Luella froze as it echoed along the quiet street.

"Luella, Bellamy will take care of him. Get into the carriage now."

The Countess was gentle but firm. She took her niece by the arm and steered her up the steps and into the phaeton's welcoming interior of comfortably upholstered velvet and polished wooden beading.

Meanwhile Bellamy was relishing every second as he stood in the hall and waited for the appropriate moment to open the front door.

Frank Connolly's hammering was ever more insistent as he straightened his jacket and passed one spade-like hand over his hair.

Pushing down the latch, he opened the door. He towered over the rather short and dumpy Frank Connolly, who was by now purple with rage.

"Where is she? I know she's in there. Step aside, man, and let me pass."

"I am sorry, sir, but I cannot admit you. There is no one at home."

"Nonsense, Luella is here, I know she is. I demand to see her!"

"There is no lady of that name in this house at this precise moment," said Bellamy truthfully. "They left for Scotland an hour or so ago."

Frank Connolly was taken aback. His mind whirled as he tried to think. Had not Jones said he had seen them at the house that afternoon at about five thirty? How could they be on their way to Scotland?

"You are lying, man, now fetch her at once, you bounder!"

Bellamy stood in the doorway so that he blocked the electric light in the passage and filled the frame. Puffing out his chest he spoke quietly, but firmly,

"Sir, they are not here. Now, I suggest you leave quietly and at once, otherwise I shall telephone the Police."

"Will you now?"

Frank Connolly squared up to the huge butler and looked him straight in the eye.

"Is everything all right, sir?"

Frank Connolly spun round to find himself staring straight at two Policemen who stood on the street behind him. His mouth fell open and words would not come.

"I am glad you are here, Officers," said Bellamy in a voice like liquid silk. "This gentleman is being aggressive and unpleasant. He is threatening to gain forceful entry into Lord Kennington's house while he is away."

The two Policemen did not hesitate. They flanked him and, with one swift movement, clapped a pair of handcuffs on him before he knew what was happening.

"If you'll just come down to the Station with us, sir."

Bellamy smiled and nodded appreciatively. Had he been forced to do so, he would have restrained Frank Connolly in any manner he saw necessary. The timely intervention of the two Police Officers was a great stroke of fortune.

"Come along, sir, do not resist arrest."

Within moments, Frank Connolly was being marched back down South Audley Street, protesting all the while at the top of his voice.

As they crossed into Mount Street, the carriage containing Luella and her aunt rounded the opposite corner. Frank Connolly paid them no heed, being too furious with the Policemen who were frogmarching him towards the Police Station.

"Well. Good riddance to Frank Connolly. Hopefully we have seen the last of him," exclaimed the Countess with thinly disguised relief.

"We are still going to Devon though aren't we?" asked Luella timidly.

"Of course, child. We cannot remain in London. No, we will take the train to Exeter. But for now Frank Connolly has got his just desserts!"

*

Much later, when they were safely ensconced on the train, Luella began to mull over in her mind what she would say to the Viscount.

'He will inevitably ask me if I have considered his proposal, but how can I accept without telling him the whole truth?'

She cast a glance at Aunt Edith who was asleep in the seat opposite. The day's events had taken their toll and she suddenly looked shockingly old.

Although nearly seventy, she had seemed so young to Luella up until that moment. As she looked at her aunt's grey face and sagging skin, she realised with a shock that she might not be around for ever.

'And she would hate not to see my wedding.'

That thought troubled Luella a great deal – she knew that it was her aunt's greatest wish to see her walk down the aisle and now she had the opportunity to grant it, should she be brave enough to do so.

'It would mean telling him everything,' she murmured, as tears sprang into her eyes. 'But I cannot keep dragging Aunt Edith all over the country and I have come to realise how much I love David.'

The train rattled on through the night lulling her to sleep. As the wheels turned and brought them ever closer to Devon, Luella made a momentous decision.

'No, I have to tell him about Jean-Marie,' she resolved. 'And tell him everything.'

CHAPTER SEVEN

Luella remained silent for a good portion of the journey. She was too busy rehearsing in her head what she would say to the Viscount.

'I wish I was as certain as Aunt Edith that David will understand about my liaison with Jean-Marie Bouillicault,' she thought. 'Men are so particular about the virtue of women and they expect those of our kind to be of flawless character. Will he think me a bad woman for having loved someone else – and to have run away with him intending to get married?'

Just before they reached Exeter, Luella awakened her aunt and helped her make herself ready for the next stage of their journey.

"Come along, Aunt Edith," she urged. "I am afraid there will be no more sleep until we reach Torr House."

"I do hope that Bennett brings some large cushions," she replied. "The Daimler can be a little uncomfortable – do you remember the journey to Barnstaple?"

"Yes," answered Luella with a little laugh. She was trying her best to remain cheerful and she did not want her aunt worrying unduly about her.

'It should be the other way around,' thought Luella. 'She is an old woman and I should be taking care of her. I forget how old she is because she is so sprightly. It is not right that, because of Frank Connolly, she has been forced to be the strong one.'

Luella was neither delicate of constitution nor weak of mind or body, but the whole business with Jean-Marie Bouillicault and then Frank Connolly had considerably depleted her.

She longed for stability and to be taken care of, and she knew that the Viscount could offer her both.

The train eventually pulled into Exeter station and the guard helped them find a porter to carry their small amount of luggage.

As promised Bennett was waiting for them on the platform.

"Good evening, my Lady and Miss Ridgeway," he said bowing. "Welcome to Devon again – and, so soon."

"Yes, I am afraid it was not planned, but nevertheless, here we are," said the Countess, as brightly as she could given that she was exhausted.

They trooped out of the station to where the Daimler was waiting for them.

The porter helped with the two suitcases and then Bennett settled his two passengers into their seats and threw blankets over their knees. The car was open to the elements but, thankfully, it was a fine and warm July night.

The drive to Bideford was long and arduous.

The dawn broke as they reached the westerly outskirts of Exmoor and by the time that Torr House came into view, the sun was rising.

Everywhere was deadly quiet apart from the lowing of cows on the hillside nearby and a distant cockerel crowing.

Luella looked at the house and it seemed unlikely that the Viscount was up yet.

'I doubt if even the servants are awake,' she mumbled,

as the car shook them from side to side, negotiating the rough drive that led to the front entrance.

The Countess groaned as they hit a large pothole and the car flew up in the air, landing with a bone-shaking thud.

When Bennett finally applied the handbrake, both Luella and the Countess breathed a sigh of relief.

'If I am aching, I cannot imagine how Aunt Edith must feel,' thought Luella, as Bennett helped her out of the Daimler.

They were all dusty and tired. How Bennett appeared so lively was beyond her comprehension.

Luella was shocked to see the Viscount striding out of the front door towards them. His shirt was flapping loose over his trousers and his sleeves were rolled back to just above his elbows.

She could not help but catch a brief glimpse of his bare chest as his shirt blew open.

Blushing, she cast her eyes downwards in order to stop herself from staring, but the sight stirred her in a manner that was both startling and unfamiliar.

"Luella," called the Viscount running towards her. If he had been able, he would have thrown his arms around her and held her fast, but he could not do so in front of the servants.

"You are safe now. All will be well."

She looked so fragile and exhausted that he could not prevent himself putting one arm around her delicate shoulders.

Luella felt the warmth of his arm through her linen jacket and almost swooned as she inhaled his masculine odour.

Walking up the front steps, she stumbled slightly and his arm slipped down to her waist while his grip tightened.

"Come, your rooms are ready for you. It is indeed fortunate that the builders have not begun work on the house as yet as they are still constructing the orangery."

Luella did not reply. She simply looked up into his handsome face and smiled.

It was an effort simply placing one foot in front of the other and she was glad of him to lean on as they mounted the stairs to the river room.

"Maisie will look after your aunt and I will employ a new maid for you at once," he said. "You are to stay here as long as you wish, that is, if you can stand the noise and dirt of the builders."

"Right now, I would not care if you hired a military band to play at the foot of the stairs – I do believe I would sleep through it," replied Luella yawning.

"Then, I shall leave you in peace."

The Viscount took her hand and kissed it fervently.

Luella felt a shiver run through her as the warmth of his lips touched her skin.

"I am so glad you have returned," he murmured unable to keep the passion from his voice. "Even if the circumstances are less than ideal. You must have been very afraid when Frank Connolly found you, but we shall speak more of this later. I will allow you to rest now."

"Thank you," replied Luella, gazing up at him with her wide blue eyes.

The Viscount would have kissed her soft lips right then and there had she not looked so tired and frail.

'It will have to wait,' he said to himself, as with his head spinning he returned to his room.

*

Luella did not wake until it was almost time for

luncheon. At first, when she opened her eyes, she was not certain where she was.

Then she remembered.

'I am safe and far away from that awful Frank Connolly.'

She recalled her last sighting of him, being propelled down Mount Street by two Policemen and allowed herself to smile.

Getting up and putting on a dressing gown, she rang for Maisie and pulled back the curtains.

She noted with satisfaction that the gardens were beginning to look halfway decent and that one of the gardeners was busy with a rose bush beneath her window.

'I shall repay the Viscount for his kindness by joining them in the garden,' she resolved. 'I shall enjoy feeling the earth running through my fingers again.'

Presently Maisie came to her room and helped her wash and dress.

"His Lordship is waiting for you in the dining room," she said, as she finished dressing Luella's lustrous hair.

"Oh?"

"He is expecting you, miss."

"He has told you this?"

"Yes, miss."

Luella felt her heart begin to race. She swallowed hard as she rose from the dressing table.

"Tell him I shall be down at once," she said in a small voice.

As soon as Maisie had left the room, Luella began to pace up and down.

'I shall tell him everything, I must,' she repeated over and over again. 'He is certain to ask me if I have considered his proposal and Aunt Edith will never forgive me if I turn him down again.'

Taking a deep breath to calm her nerves, she walked slowly downstairs and into the dining room.

The Viscount had changed his clothes and was looking extremely handsome.

"Your aunt sends her apologies," he began as he seated her at the table. "She has a headache from the long journey."

As he stood over her, he longed to touch her shining golden hair or caress the white neck that rose up from her lawn gown.

He knew that he must ask her again if she would marry him or he would go mad from the suspense.

"I often forget that Aunt Edith is no longer young," replied Luella as Cork came into the room and greeted her warmly.

"Welcome back, Miss Ridgeway," he said as he poured a glass of water for her. "Everyone is most happy to see you and her Ladyship again."

Cork brought the luncheon to the table and the Viscount started to discuss the gardens with her. He was far too nervous to broach the subject of marriage so early in the conversation.

Eventually, as the meal drew to a close, he knew he would have to take his courage in both hands and ask the question burning inside him.

Clearing his throat, he said,

"I was wondering if you have had the opportunity to consider my proposal."

Luella put down her dessertspoon and could not meet his eyes.

He noticed that she seemed hesitant to speak and believed the worst.

"I have," she responded at last in her clear musical voice. "But after what I am about to tell you, you may wish to consider whether or not to withdraw it."

"*Never*," he cried, his brown eyes burning. "Why would I do such a thing?"

"Because," mumbled Luella quietly. "I was once engaged – to another."

The Viscount's heart was now beating so furiously it made his breathing difficult.

"Is that all?" he spluttered. "It is of no consequence – it does not present any impediment to our becoming engaged."

"But, I – I am second-hand goods."

"You mean – ?"

"*No*. My virtue is intact, but the fact is – I ran away with him. We were to be married."

The Viscount rose from the table and sank down beside her. Taking her hand, he turned her face towards him with a tender gesture and his warm brown eyes sought hers.

"Luella. I say again – it is of no consequence."

"But this man caused a great scandal in France as he was already married. I was so ashamed I thought I would die. It was reported in the newspapers although I was not named."

The Viscount swallowed hard. He loved her so much that even if there had been some impropriety, he would not have cared.

As he knelt besides her, all he wanted to do was embrace her and kiss her.

"Luella, it does not matter to me in the least. You are who you are and I love you dearly. This man has made you feel as if you were worthless, has he not?"

"Yes. I believed that no decent man would ever have

me. When I first met Frank Connolly, I admit I was a little flattered by his attentions and so did not spurn him. Of course later he became more persistent and troublesome, but I believed I had brought it upon myself.

"When he said we should marry, I found it impossible to shake him off. He knew of the situation with Jean-Marie and threatened to ruin my family's name should I not comply."

"He is a bully and a coward! Such men are no better than animals – "

"But – " began Luella, but she was silenced by the Viscount wrapping his arms around her and kissing her sweet mouth over and over again.

As they parted the Viscount caressed her cheek and sighed.

"Oh, Luella. I love you so very much. Nothing you can say will put me off marrying you, *so will you?*"

He pulled away from her and knelt before her clasping her hand in his.

"Say *yes*, Luella. Do me the honour of becoming my wife."

Tears sprang into Luella's eyes as she watched him, kneeling so earnestly before her.

She did not think, but simply said what was in her heart.

"*I will*," she murmured. "For I love you too."

"Luella, my darling," he cried, getting up and pulling her to her feet in a warm and passionate embrace.

He could not believe that at last she was in his arms.

As their lips parted, she clung to his chest like a small animal, burrowing there for safety. It made him feel incredibly protective towards her and he knew that, from now on, it was his duty to keep her safe from harm.

"I cannot believe I could be so happy," he murmured as he cradled her in his arms. "You have made me the happiest man alive."

"I thought I did not deserve love."

"Why? Because you had the misfortune to fall in love with a man who did not deserve you?"

"I thought God would punish me for the rest of my days," muttered Luella as he kissed her hair gently.

His heart swelled as she spoke and he held her even more tightly.

"God does not judge you for falling in love. Rather he punishes those who do not realise the importance of love."

"But who could fail to understand that?" queried Luella in disbelief.

"I used to believe that love was unimportant," admitted the Viscount, begging her with his eyes to not think ill of him.

Just then there came a knock on the door.

"That will be Cork," said the Viscount. "I asked him to leave us alone after serving coffee."

Luella laughed and it was music to his ears.

"I had wondered where he had gone to. That was very crafty of you."

"I knew that I had to press you for an answer or die. Now, I should admit Cork and then go and see your aunt. As your father is no longer with us, she will serve as the next best thing."

"You are to ask my aunt for my hand?" asked Luella incredulous.

"Of course. It is how things are done and besides I cannot help but feel your aunt will be delighted to be consulted in such vital matters. She loves you a great deal and is as a second mother to you."

"Yes, you are right. I do not know what I would have done without her kindness. She took me in when no one else would."

Taking Luella's hand the Viscount led her towards the blue room.

Upon knocking and entering they found Aunt Edith sitting by the window enjoying her luncheon.

"Aunt, has your headache gone already?"

"It turned out to be not as serious as I had first thought," she replied smiling.

"Lady Ridgeway, I have something to ask you," began the Viscount. "I have asked Luella to marry me and she has accepted. Now, we come to ask your permission to marry."

The Countess clapped her hands together in delight.

"Oh, Luella! Did I not say that all would be well? Of course, Lord Kennington, you have my blessing."

"Please, you must call me David. After all, we shall soon be part of each other's families."

"David, I am so thrilled," said the Countess, rising to embrace first him and then Luella.

"Some champagne is in order, I believe."

"What, in the afternoon?" queried Luella.

"Why ever not?"

"My thoughts precisely," added the Countess, moving towards the bell.

Later, when Cork had brought a bottle of what had once been one of Madame Le Fevre's favourite vintages, he smiled to himself as the pop resounded.

'Madame would have been very happy to see this day,' he thought to himself, as he closed the door on the celebrating trio. 'She always said that this house was full of love and now it's that way once more.'

That evening at dinner, Luella expressed her wish to work in the garden.

"It would be a way of thanking you for everything you have done for us."

"But you are now my fiancée, you do not have to thank me for anything. We should both be thanking the Lord that He has brought us together."

He took her hand across the table and kissed it.

On the third finger sparkled a large emerald surrounded by small diamonds.

A part of him felt very sad that his father and grandmother were not there to share the moment with him.

He had begun to write secretly to his grandmother each week and had Cork or Mrs. Cork address the envelope so that his father would not recognise the hand and destroy it before it reached her.

Now he knew what his next letter would contain – how he had found love and was engaged to be married.

"When will the wedding be?" asked the Countess. "Have you given any thought to a date or place?"

"I think we are both of the same mind that as our love flowered here in Devon, this is where we shall be wed," answered the Viscount.

"Will you invite your family?"

"I do not think that Papa would lower himself to attend my wedding and enter the house of his father's mistress!"

The Countess hid a smile. She had encountered many such arrangements in France, but here in England it was still frowned on.

"I understand you would not wish to remind your grandmother that she was not the only woman in her late husband's life," she replied. "But surely, she would wish to see you happily married? She does not have to come to the house after all."

"If it were down to Grandmama, she would most likely bend, but Papa. Never."

As Cork opened another bottle of champagne, Luella's mind was busy forming a scheme. If there was any way she could come to his rescue, then what better way to repay his kindness?

'Yes,' she mumbled to herself. 'I do believe I shall be writing to the Dowager Marchioness before too long.'

*

The weeks passed quickly and July became August.

Luella threw herself into landscaping the gardens, although it was too early to start the spring planting.

Meanwhile, the builders had completed the orangery, while work on the main house was gathering pace.

The noise and the dust were tremendous, so when the Countess announced at breakfast one morning, that she intended to return to Braemore Castle, Luella was not surprised.

"Will you not stay a little longer, Aunt?" asked Luella. "Although the wedding is not until the end of September, there is still so much to accomplish."

"You have all these new servants to help," said the Countess, alluding to Grace, Luella's new lady's maid. "And I can telephone from Scotland if more help is needed. You are after all not having a large and grand wedding."

"Judging by the amount of visitors to the house this week, you should not let the local people here you say that," retorted the Viscount laughing. "It will be the most important event of the year in Bideford. We may not have many family attending, but the list of people from the area who have been invited grows daily."

"That is because you invite each and every person who calls at the house," said Luella fondly. "But it is a pity that your Papa and Grandmama will not be attending. Is there no chance of a reconciliation before the day?"

"None, Luella. My father blames me for Grandpapa's death and even Grandmama cannot persuade him otherwise."

Luella did not tell him that she had written to the Dowager Marchioness at the house in Belgrave Square that very morning. She hoped that the old lady would receive her letter and that the Earl would not destroy it should he catch sight of the postmark.

And so a few days later Bennett was loading up the Daimler with the Countess's bags.

"Is there any of your things you would like me send to you from Scotland?" she asked, as they stood on the steps of Torr House in the hot August sun.

"No, Aunt Edith. I do not wish to be reminded of my former life. I must only look to the future from now on. Besides, when I visit the dressmaker later this afternoon for the fitting of my wedding dress, she is giving me a number of dresses and suits she has made up for me."

"Everyone is delighted at Luella's patronage of local businesses," said the Viscount putting his arm around her. "She has become the most popular young lady in this part of the County."

"It's true," sighed Luella. "I have not worked as much as I had hoped in the garden, because every day there is someone else calling to see me and I have made so many new friends."

"And I expect the article in the *North Devon Journal* last week about Bideford's great Society wedding that informed everyone that you were to have your wedding dress made here, rather than London, has also precipitated the march to your door," smiled the Countess. "I am glad you have settled in so well."

"But I will you miss you so much, Aunt Edith. Are you quite sure you will not change your mind?"

"No, dearest. The noise and the dust are too much for me to bear and I prefer the cooler climate of my Scottish home at this time of year."

She kissed Luella goodbye and Bennett helped her into the Daimler.

Luella began to cry as the motor car roared into life and was almost sobbing by the time that it disappeared down the drive.

'Goodbye, Aunt Edith,' she whispered, when she could no longer see the Daimler. 'The next time I will see you will be on my wedding day.'

*

The Earl of Kennington was in a very good mood. So far that evening, he had won three games and now he looked at the Royal Flush in his hands and felt very pleased with himself.

"No, it's no good. Luck is against me tonight!"

The ruddy-faced fellow opposite him threw down his cards and had to bear the sight of the pile of coins in front of him being scooped up by the jubilant Earl.

"Another game, Connolly?" he suggested, lighting a large Havana cigar.

"Not for me, Lord Kennington. But I would be happy to buy you a brandy if you would do me the honour of joining me in the bar."

The Earl laughed.

"You are a glutton for punishment," he said rising from the table. "First I fleece you and then you offer to buy me a drink."

"I have enough to stand a round," protested Frank Connolly. He did not want the Earl to leave, as he had not yet extricated the information from him he so dearly wanted.

"Very well, but I shall buy the brandy," exclaimed the Earl, clapping him on the back. "Any fellow who takes his losses so well deserves a reward."

The two walked through the dimly lit panelled rooms of the gaming house to a quiet bar. The Earl had taken to frequenting it a great deal in the past few months since his father had died, now with an enviable fortune to fritter away, it took his mind off other less pleasant matters.

As they passed the tables playing all manner of high-stake card games, through the plumes of cigar and cigarette smoke, Frank Connolly congratulated himself on a fine piece of detective work.

'That fool Jones cost me a great deal of money and he could not find me Luella,' he thought, as the Earl sat down and ordered two glasses of cognac. 'It took my own ingenuity to track down the Viscount's father and befriend him.'

"Damn fine cognac, eh? Makes one forget life's troubles."

The Earl savoured the rich aroma that rose from his glass and sipped at it with his eyes closed.

"Your son – you are still estranged from him?"

Frank Connolly knew he was risking his new friendship by broaching a personal matter, but had it not been alluded to at the card table that evening?

Lord Portchester had brought up the topic of conversation when he had asked if he might borrow a team of horses that belonged to the Viscount, only to be told in no uncertain terms that it would not be possible.

"Yes," answered the Earl taking another sip of cognac.

"It's a terrible thing for a father to be at war with his son."

"My son was the reason for my own father's sudden expiration," said the Earl, bitterly. "He is dead as far as I am concerned."

"He is no longer in London?"

"No, he is in Bideford in North Devon in a house that used to belong to my father. Good job, too. Best place for him!"

Frank Connolly took a deep draught of the cognac and smiled to himself with immense satisfaction.

'So, the Viscount is in Bideford,' he thought, as the Earl sat smoking in silence. 'I should have guessed that Luella would be holed up in some house of his.'

After a while, Frank Connolly pronounced himself tired and shook the Earl by the hand.

"Shall we play a hand tomorrow evening?" asked the Earl.

"I am afraid not. I leave London in the morning."

"Off for the shooting?"

Frank Connolly put on his hat and smiled.

"It has been a pleasure, sir. Perhaps we will meet again the next time I am in London?"

The Earl grunted his assent and clicked his fingers at a waiter who was passing by with a tray.

Frank Connolly left immediately. He had much to do before the morning.

'To think I wasted time on a wild goose chase to Scotland,' he said to himself, 'but it was money well spent. I feel in my bones that Luella must be hiding in Devon. If she thought she had seen the last of me, she is very much mistaken!'

*

The next morning, Frank Connolly did not waste any time. He packed his suitcase and set off for Paddington station.

Having ascertained that the only way to Bideford was via Exeter, he withdrew funds from his father's bank in Piccadilly to cover his expenses.

'I shall not need a great deal,' he told himself. 'As soon as I have married Luella, we shall return to Ireland and show my father that I have made something of myself. Won't he be surprised to find that I have forged a liaison with one of the most powerful families in Scotland? And our children will be rich and important.'

He visibly puffed himself out at the thought. All his life had been the youngest son of a minor Irish Lord of little or no significance in the eyes of Society.

'And once the old girl is in her coffin, I will become a force to be reckoned with and, through Luella's wealth, I will enjoy a fine standard of living.'

By the time he eventually reached Bideford, he had already imagined himself to be Laird of all he surveyed and that the Earl would greet him as an equal, not someone to beat at cards.

He quickly found himself a decent hotel and settled himself down in the bar to wait for the restaurant to open. He was famished after his long journey.

Before long he knew he would have to start making enquiries to find the house where Luella was staying. As he sipped his whisky, he idly picked up a local newspaper that someone had left behind.

It was then that he saw it in the Society pages.

His eyes bulged with fury as he read the article entitled *The wedding of the year*, which spoke of a Miss Luella Ridgeway of Braemore Castle, Perthshire, who was marrying Viscount Kennington, the new owner of Torr House, in September.

"*The bride has made many friends in Bideford by making the decision to have her wedding gown and trousseau made at Mrs. Clarke's establishment in Market Street,*" it read. "*The dress, we are told, will be embellished with Honiton lace and will be, no doubt, the talk of Devon.*"

'How dare she!' he spluttered, throwing the newspaper away in disgust. 'She *cannot* marry another. If she thinks she is marrying this Viscount, she is very much mistaken. I can see that time is no longer on my side, so I must find my way to this Torr House and take her back to London at once.'

He drained his glass and returned straight to his room, his appetite vanished.

His suitcase lay on the bed where he had left it. Slowly he opened it and took out all the clothes, and then he pulled out something heavy wrapped in a black cloth and weighed it in his hand.

With a swift movement he unravelled the bundle to reveal a pistol.

'Yes,' he murmured, as he polished the gun with the cloth it had been wrapped in. 'This Viscount is a fool if he thinks he can steal the woman who belongs to me. If I have to kill him to get Luella back, then so be it!'

CHAPTER EIGHT

Luella knelt by the raised flower bed and diligently plucked the weeds from it, making certain that she left none behind. The sun beat down upon her back and she felt a sense of enormous contentment.

Just along from her, Thomas and Johnny were busy digging a new bed that was on a patch of land once occupied by a recently demolished outbuilding.

Luella reflected that her life was almost perfect.

'But that day will come when David and I are married,' she thought with a satisfied smile.

She missed her Aunt Edith a great deal as it was the first time since she had been to Finishing School that she was not at her side. Although they wrote to each other frequently and spoke on the telephone, it was not the same.

The Countess wrote eloquently of the comings and goings at Braemore Castle and commented that the raspberries were doing very well.

"Pardon me, my Lady, but would you come and supervise the planting of the bedding?"

Both Thomas and Johnny always referred to Luella as 'my Lady', even though until the day that the Viscount's wedding ring was on her finger, she would not be entitled to it.

"Of course, Thomas," she said, getting up and dusting off her hands.

She knew that Aunt Edith would have been very cross with her for not wearing gloves, but Luella loved to feel the earth as she worked.

She wore her engagement ring on a sturdy gold chain around her neck until the time she washed her hands and could return it to her finger with a sense of pride.

Johnny walked towards them carrying a tray of bedding plants already in bloom.

"Where shall I put these, my Lady?"

"I think the marigolds should be placed at the edges of each area and then fill in with the zinnias."

She fumbled in her apron and brought out a sketchbook with her designs.

"Yes," she said finding the relevant page. "And next we shall plant the standard rose bushes in the middle of each bed in the autumn."

Luella and the gardeners worked happily away completely unaware that a shadow had fallen over Bideford.

*

In the Red Lion Hotel, Frank Connolly was busy talking to whomever he could find in order to discover more about the Viscount and where he lived.

"Oh, he be the London gent who inherited the Frenchwoman's old house," said the ancient doorman. "He's made a lot of friends hereabouts by employing local tradesmen to rebuild the place. And then there's that wedding – Bideford ain't seen the like of it for many a long year."

"Do you know when it is?" asked Frank Connolly, slipping the man a shilling.

"End of September – the twenty-ninth, if I rightly recall.

They say that no one from London is coming which is mighty strange, mighty – "

The doorman shook his head and Frank Connolly thanked the man before striding out into the street.

From the enquiries he had made so far, it was not going to be difficult to find the Viscount's house. Everyone had said that it could be seen from the river and that it was situated on the main road out of Bideford heading West.

"Torr House?" they had said. "You cannot miss it."

He climbed the steep hill towards the market and looked for the chemist's shop that the doorman had told him about.

He had certain items he wished to buy.

At last at the very brow of the hill he found it. He walked inside and purchased a bottle of chloroform. He told the chemist he was a keen collector of butterflies.

"In that case, will you be needing lint pads as well?"

'It is as if the Gods are on my side' thought Connolly with a self-satisfied air, as he left the shop and walked back down the hill.

The chemist had been more than helpful. When asked if there might be any disused buildings that might harbour a rare Camberwell Beauty, the man had directed him to an old shepherd's hut on the outskirts of the town.

"I could not say if you will find one up there," said the chemist. "But I know that other lepidopterists have found many rare and collectible species there. It is quiet and rarely visited and is plentifully stocked with the kind of plants they love."

He had even been so good as to provide him with a rough sketch on a piece of brown paper where he might find the building.

Without pausing to drop off his purchases, Frank

Connolly set out on the long walk to the shepherd's hut. It was quite difficult to find and he almost gave up when he became hot and tired.

But a chance encounter with a farm worker pointed him in the right direction.

The hut was just what he desired. Inside was a room with an intact door that he judged he could wedge shut with a dirty wooden chair he had found outside.

'Or I could go to the ironmonger's in town and buy some locks and chains,' he debated as he looked around the hut. 'It is good that there are no windows that she can escape from.'

Later as he made a mental list of items to buy to put his plan into action, he returned to the hotel and ate a hearty dinner.

'Tomorrow after I have made the hut ready, I will go to Torr House and see if I can spy Luella,' he mumbled, as the waiter took away his plate. 'And if conditions are favourable, I will return to take her away.'

*

"David, you really must ask the builders not to dump masonry on the flower beds," complained Luella, as she entered the dining room for breakfast the next day.

The Viscount was already seated at the table and put down the copy of *The Times* he had been reading.

"I will speak to Mr. Pensworth at once."

"Thank you, darling."

Luella kissed him on the forehead and took her place at the table. At once, Cork set down a teacup and saucer alongside a rack of toast.

"I want to start with the herbs soon and poor Thomas and Johnny have dug that bed twice already. But the builders will insist on dropping bricks all over it. It really will not do once we have planted the seedlings."

"He shall be told as soon as I have finished breakfast."

He looked over at Luella and thought how she was blossoming by the day.

'If I had thought her beautiful when I first met her, then now she is a veritable Goddess amongst women,' he said to himself. 'The country air suits her and she has gained a little weight. I shall be the proudest man in England the day I wait for her at the altar.'

Cork came in with the morning post. As always, Luella hoped fervently that the Marchioness had written a reply to her letter. But so far there had been no response.

Cork set down the silver salver by the Viscount and she realised with a sigh that there was nothing for her today.

'Perhaps she is not in London,' she thought, as she buttered a slice of toast. 'There is the house in the country after all – or maybe they have gone to Biarritz."

Luella resolved to write again enclosing an invitation to the wedding. She knew that the Viscount would be overjoyed if his grandmother could attend their special day.

"What are you doing today, Luella?" he asked. "More gardening? If you are not careful, you will soon be as brown as a field hand and everyone will think that my bride-to-be is either a foreigner or a fruit-picker!"

Luella laughed.

It was true. Her hands and arms had begun to tan, in spite of wearing a large-brimmed hat. She spread them out before her and thought that, if she was here, Aunt Edith would tick her off for not covering herself more efficiently.

"I shall ask Mrs. Cork to buy some lemons so that I can whiten my skin with the juice," she remarked. "The weather has been so glorious this past week that it has been too hot to wear long sleeves."

"My little nut-brown gypsy!" he teased, getting up and nuzzling her hair. "It is a good job that my Mama is not still alive, as she would have been scandalised by a lady working in her own garden."

"It is, I believe, the most genteel of pastimes."

"Not when the lady in question is matching the gardeners for the amount of heavy work she is doing. I wonder where you get your strength from."

"Aunt Edith says it is my good Scottish blood."

"Then, I pray you will pass that blood on and we will have good strong sons."

He kissed her goodbye and vanished outside to speak to the builders. Luella passed her hand over her cheeks and found them burning.

'*Children*,' she murmured.

She thought of her aunt's last letter in which she had lectured her on a woman's marital duties.

Luella was both scared and thrilled at the thought that soon she and the Viscount would find themselves in each other's arms after they had said goodnight.

"Do not be frightened of the physical side of marriage," her aunt had counselled. "Far from being the terrible torture that some would make you believe it to be, it is, in the right man's arms, like touching Heaven itself."

It was true that the Viscount had awoken a burning desire in her that she had never felt before, not even with Jean-Marie Bouillicault.

She remained at the breakfast table, dreaming of the walk she had taken in the gardens with the Viscount the previous evening.

When he had taken her in his arms under the full moon and kissed her, she had felt something wild and tumultuous unleashed in her that had made her respond enthusiastically to his caresses.

'I would dearly love to experience what Aunt Edith calls 'touching Heaven',' she sighed. 'And I know that David is indeed the right man.'

Her reverie was interrupted by Grace, informing her that the dressmaker had arrived for her fitting.

'There is still so much to do,' she thought as she followed Grace upstairs.

*

Later, after luncheon, Luella donned her old clothes and went out into the garden. A very contrite Mr. Pensworth had come and apologised for the mess his men had made and had offered to clear the beds completely for her.

She hurried to the beds and found Johnny and Thomas supervising two labourers as they ferried wheelbarrows full of rich new earth to the area.

"Good afternoon, my Lady," said Thomas. "With this fine soil we shall be able to plant the seedlings and the shrubs at once."

"Excellent," replied Luella.

Once the labourers had finished tipping the new soil onto the beds, Johnny brought seedlings and a selection of rosemary, lavender and verbena bushes. Thomas took trays of tiny camomile plants and placed them in a good sunny site.

"Yes, I think Mrs. Cork will soon be harvesting a modest amount of herbs for the dinner table," she said, stroking the delicate fern of a fennel plant.

"Pardon me, my Lady, but can we go up to the terrace and look at the old japonica?" asked Johnny. "If we're going to move it, then we should decide on where it's going."

"Of course. Thomas, can you manage here?"

"Yes, my Lady."

Luella followed Johnny through the kitchen garden until they reached the far edge of the gardens.

A large japonica had survived there and Luella fingered the glossy green leaves and noticed signs that it could possibly flower this year.

"We should not move it until it has finished flowering next spring," she remarked. "Johnny, would you go to the potting shed and bring the insect spray? There are signs of infestation around the buds and we should treat it now."

Johny touched his cap and lumbered off down the slope.

Luella bent down to pull out a patch of weeds.

'This weeding is never done,' she sighed, pulling out handfuls of chickweed.

*

As Frank Connolly crept along the drive of Torr House, he instinctively stroked the hard outline of the gun inside his jacket.

He had stood at the gates for some time before starting on the long walk towards the house.

It had been simplicity itself for him to find the house. He had crossed the bridge, walked for a while and then, there it was!

"If everything else goes as smoothly as things have done so far, then Luella and I will be on our way to Ireland by the morning," he said out loud.

He planned to hire a carriage and have it drive them both to Liverpool and from there they would take the ferry to Dublin.

He would wire his father and ask for a carriage to meet them and to have the Priest ready to marry him and Luella in the family Chapel on the estate at Kilsharry.

He had now reached the end of the drive. In front of

him, he could see the heavy front door of the Jacobean building and its tessellated windows. One side of the house was clad in scaffolding and there was a builder's cart in front of the house.

'I did not expect there to be so many people around,' he said to himself, as he crept nearer and waited. 'But that man has stolen Luella from me and *he has to pay.*'

He realised that it would now be a great deal more difficult to abduct Luella without being seen. He cursed his ill-fortune and remained crouched behind a hedge.

As he did so, Bennett came roaring up in the Daimler. With a swift movement, he stopped the car and applied the handbrake. Whistling, he jumped out and entered the house.

Immediately Frank Connolly was struck by an idea.

'If I take the motor car, I could take Luella away much more speedily than if I used a horse and cart. And the stupid fool appears to have left the keys in it.'

He felt as if something or someone else had taken over his body as he moved stealthily towards it. He had some experience of driving motor cars and had once driven this very same model.

With a quick look around to see that no one was about, he crept over to the car, jumped in and started it up. Still no one came out to scc what was going on.

Moving forward, he followed some old tyre tracks that led around the side of the house.

'It must be time for the builders break,' he thought, as he noticed the empty scaffolding and abandoned wheelbarrows.

Within moments, he was driving along the track that ran alongside the gardens.

Suddenly he heard voices.

He stopped the car and got out. Behind a newly built

wall, he could clearly hear Luella talking to someone. Moving slowly forwards, he crept along the wall until he came to a gate.

"Thank you, Johnny. You may go and have your luncheon now," he heard Luella say.

'This is my chance,' he thought, as he put his hand on the bottle of chloroform in his pocket. 'What great fortune.'

He peeped around the garden gate and saw Luella walking away. His heart lurched as he watched her, so happy in the sunshine and then he grew angry.

'How dare that man steal her from me!' he fumed, working himself into a rage.

He waited for a while to make sure that the coast was clear and then he moved stealthily towards Luella. In his hand he carried a pad soaked in chloroform.

She was kneeling down, pulling at weeds when, all of a sudden, she felt a hand clap around her mouth and then all went black.

Frank Connolly lifted her limp figure up into his arms and headed for the motor car. He pushed Luella into the passenger seat and bound her feet and hands.

"You will not escape from me now," he muttered covering her with a blanket.

But the Daimler had decided to be temperamental. It took several cranks of the handle before the engine coughed into life. By then he was sweating profusely and his heart was hammering fit to burst.

Further down the garden, he heard the shouts of the builders returning to work.

'Curse it!' he mumbled. 'I shall have to be quick otherwise someone might apprehend us.'

Turning round he saw to his delight that the chauffeur had left his cap on the rear seat of the motor car.

Immediately, he tore off his own hat and replaced it with the chauffeur's cap.

'Now, I shall have to make haste to get up enough speed before I reach the front entrance and we can sail past without anyone noticing. They will simply think Luella has gone for a drive with her chauffeur.'

He pressed his foot down hard on the accelerator and the engine roared. Letting out the clutch, it rocketed forwards.

The ground was uneven as they bounced along the drive.

As he rounded the corner, he saw the Viscount standing outside the house with his back to the road.

With a grim expression he pressed the accelerator down further and the motor car gathered speed.

As the Viscount was so preoccupied talking to the builders, he did not at first pay any heed to the vehicle as it sped behind him.

But then one of the builders made a remark that made him turn round.

"That chauffeur o' yorn is in a right 'urry," he exclaimed with an envious smile on his face.

The Viscount frowned as he had told Bennett to drive with caution along the rough drive. He did not wish to pay for expensive repairs to the suspension – or worse.

Spinning on his heel, he caught sight of the Daimler shrouded in a cloud of dust that obscured both the driver and passenger.

It crossed his mind that maybe Luella was in the motor car with Bennett, but did not give it any further thought.

Frank Connolly drove as fast as he could to the shepherd's hut. He was fortunate that he encountered very little other traffic on the road, as he was wary of drawing attention to himself.

'Everyone will know the Viscount's Daimler,' he thought. 'And if someone sees a stranger driving it, they might go and raise the alarm.'

But in the blistering August sun, most were either asleep in the hay or inside taking refuge from the hot weather.

It did not take him long to reach the hut. He had returned there that morning to prepare it for his visit.

First he had fixed a padlock to the door of the inner room and had taken the wooden chair inside.

'I shall have to tie Luella to it,' he thought. 'Until such time as I have disposed of that Viscount.'

Luella groaned in the seat next to him. She was beginning to come round.

Quickly he picked her up and carried her inside the hut just as she regained consciousness.

"Where am I?" she murmured groggily.

Then she saw Frank Connolly's red face next to hers and she tried to scream, but found that she was too weak to do so.

"Be quiet, Luella," he demanded. "And do not struggle."

She could not understand why she could not move her arms or legs, then she realised that he had bound her.

He pushed her into the chair and swiftly secured her by winding a rope around her body and the chair.

"Do not try to move and do not give me any trouble," he warned her, standing back and viewing her tethered and helpless.

"Why are you doing this?" she howled at him beginning to cry.

She felt sick and her mind would not function.

All she knew that it was Frank Connolly who had

taken her and now she was his prisoner. She could not even remember where she had been or what had happened after everything had gone black.

"You know why. You are mine! *Mine*, you hear? And you can forget about this ridiculous wedding to this Viscount," he spat. "We are going to Ireland and we shall be married the moment we reach Kilsharry!"

"But I am marrying David! You cannot make me marry you. He will come looking for me."

"He does not even know you have gone," he sneered. "And by the time he does, I will have taken care of him."

A cold hand of fear gripped at Luella's heart.

"What do you mean?"

Frank Connolly turned his back on her and put his hand inside his jacket. His fingers sought out the hard barrel of the gun and he smiled with satisfaction.

"David will be out looking for me. There is not an inch of this country that his men don't know – they will find me and you will be thrown into jail," shrieked Luella, her voice rising in sheer panic.

She realised that Frank Connolly was not in his right mind and now she was terrified of what he was going to do next.

"Shut up!" he retorted sharply. "That man is no match for *me*."

"He will see you put away for a very long time. Of that, you can be certain."

Frank Connolly turned and laughed in her face – a cruel, hard laugh.

"Not if I get to him first. I shall make certain he does not live to put me into prison."

He took out his pistol and waved it in Luella's face.

"You – *cannot*," she whimpered, tears streaming down her face.

Without saying another word, he took out the bottle of chloroform and wetted a lint pad with it.

"Do I have to use this again?" he roared.

Luella shook her head sadly and became compliant.

He left the room and locked the padlock firmly behind him.

The room was dark and windowless and as soon as the door closed, she was plunged into semi-darkness. A thin ray of light penetrated underneath the foot of the door and illuminated the filth on the floor.

Luella hung her head and wept silently. She did not wish to give him the satisfaction of breaking down.

"Oh, David. Help me! *Help me!*" she repeated over and over again, as if by repetition her message would somehow get through to him.

Frank Connolly sat in the driver's seat of the Daimler and silently loaded the pistol. The engine was ticking over and he knew what he now had to do.

'If that clever Viscount thinks he has got one over on me, then he is a fool!' he said through gritted teeth.

Tucking the pistol back into his jacket, he let out the clutch and the motor car moved forward.

'I shall put an end to this 'Wedding of the Year' once and for all,' he growled, as the Daimler made its way slowly to the main road.

*

At Torr House, the Viscount was sitting in the dining room awaiting Luella's arrival so that they could start luncheon.

'Where is that girl?' he muttered, as Cork brought in the plates.

"Cork, have you seen Miss Ridgeway?"

"No, my Lord. Shall I ask Thomas and Johnny? They are back in the garden again after their break."

"If you would, Cork."

But Cork returned some fifteen minutes later saying that no one had seen Miss Ridgeway since before their midday break.

"That is very strange. Perhaps that was her I saw in the car with Bennett."

"That is impossible, my Lord."

"Why do you say that, Cork?"

"Because Bennett is in the kitchen with Mrs. Cork, my Lord."

A shot of fear ran through the Viscount's body. Without a word, he leapt up from his seat and ran out of the dining room towards the back stairs.

His heart was beating wildly as he rushed into the kitchen to see a surprised Bennett and Mrs. Cork jump to their feet as he entered.

"Bennett. What are you doing here?" he cried. "I thought I saw you go out in the car not an hour ago?"

"No, my Lord. I brought the Daimler back here, as I was getting low on petrol. I was going to fill her up after lunch."

"So who was that I saw driving like a bat out of hell towards the front gates earlier then?"

Mrs. Cork and Bennett looked at each other in bewilderment and a terrible sick feeling came over the Viscount.

"Mrs. Cork, have you seen anyone unfamiliar around the house today?"

"No, my Lord."

The Viscount ran outside to where Thomas and Johnny were talking to the builders.

"I say," he shouted to them. "Has anyone seen anyone strange around the place today?"

They all shook their heads and mumbled 'no' apart from one.

"Well, when I was on the roof, I did see someone hangin' around the walled garden, my Lord. But I thought 'e was a surveyor," piped up an old man in a flat cap known as Old Ben . "At least, that's what I took 'im to be."

The Viscount moved towards the man with his heart hammering hard.

"This man, what did he look like?"

"About forty years old with a red face, my Lord. Dressed smart, he was."

Even though the Viscount had never seen Frank Connolly, he knew enough from how Luella had described him to know instinctively it was him.

And who else could it be?

"Connolly – " muttered the Viscount, as the awful truth hit him.

"Right, everyone. I have strong reason to believe that Miss Ridgeway has been kidnapped and my Daimler stolen.

"Bennett, send one of the gardeners to the Police Station in Bideford at once and raise the alarm. Tell them a Mr. Frank Connolly has abducted Miss Ridgeway and give them Old Ben's description. Everyone else, get out every last horse, carriage and cart in the place and we must go and search for her."

"They won't have gone far, my Lord. There was barely enough petrol to get to the next town and back," added Bennett.

Fifteen minutes later, the Viscount was in the gunroom

handing out a variety of pistols and shotguns. He had no idea where to begin their hunt, but was relying on the local knowledge of the men around him.

Everyone had downed tools to join in the search.

As the Viscount mounted the horse that had been made ready for him, one of the builders came to him and drew his attention to a series of tyre tracks.

"Look, my Lord," he called. "I've already followed them from the track alongside the gardens where Old Ben says he saw someone lurking and they go all the way out to the drive."

"Then, we shall follow them and they will lead us to Luella," cried the Viscount, signalling to everyone to proceed forwards.

As he rode at the head of the procession of men, he called to his love, wherever she might be.

'Luella. I am coming,' he prayed, frantic with worry. 'I will find you. *I promise you.*'

CHAPTER NINE

Frank Connolly was like a man possessed as he drove the Daimler back along the road towards Bideford. Over and over again he chanted to himself.

'He will not have her! This wedding will never take place!' until he was almost delirious with rage.

As the River Torridge came into view, the car spluttered a little as if it might stall, so he pressed down the accelerator hard and it ran smoothly once more.

Approaching the turn for Torr House, Frank Connolly brought the motor car to a halt for a moment.

It was then that he saw on the other side of the bank the procession of carts, carriages and horses headed by the Viscount.

'They are out searching for Luella already,' he thought with a mounting sense of frustration.

Taking on one man, face-to-face, was one thing, but this convoy of angry-looking men? Not even Frank Connolly was fool enough to believe that he could engage them all and not be overpowered.

With a snort he reversed the car around the corner and headed back the way he had come.

'I shall have to take Luella to Ireland without killing the Viscount,' he hissed to himself. 'Let them scour the country like fools. They shall not find where I have hidden her and we will make our escape.'

With a roar of the engine the Daimler sped back up the road towards the hut.

Luella had long since cried herself to exhaustion that tears no longer came and had resigned herself to hoping and praying that the Viscount would somehow find her.

'Surely someone will know of this place?' she whispered to herself. 'I would imagine that this hut was used by farm workers or maybe shepherds in days gone by to shelter during bad weather.'

The ropes that bound her wrists and ankles were rough and chafed her. Although she could not see, she was certain they had rubbed her flesh raw.

'And to think this morning I had not a care in the world and believed Frank Connolly was no longer a threat!'

The thin shaft of light under the door was beginning to move. Luella had no idea what time it might be, but she was becoming hungry and thirsty.

'Oh, David, rescue me, help me. I need you desperately,' she prayed over and over again.

It was yet another hot day and the temperature was beginning to rise.

'He will never get away with this,' she told herself in order to keep her spirits up. 'Does he really believe that he can come to a part of the country that he does not know and outwit David's staff who have lived here all their lives? Of course, they will know of this place and will think of it eventually – '

And when she heard the sound of a motor vehicle pulling up outside the hut, she hoped against hope that it would not be Frank Connolly returning.

'He could not have driven to Torr House and killed David in such a short time,' she agonised. And even though she was terrified, that slim ray of hope made her feel a little better.

She then heard a fearful crashing around outside the hut and then there came the sound of the padlock being undone.

The next thing she saw was Frank Connolly's angry face as he pushed the door open with great force.

"There has been a change of plan," he bellowed.

Luella noticed that he appeared agitated. It was, she thought, as if he did not really know what to do next.

He came up behind her and undid the ropes that bound her to the chair.

"Are you letting me go free?" she asked hopefully.

"Don't be stupid," he yelled, the colour mounting once more in his chubby face. "That damned Viscount is heading up a search party for you and I almost drove straight into their path. No, we are going to drive to Liverpool and catch the ferry."

"Liverpool! But the Daimler – "

"Shut up and do as I say, unless you want me to hurt you or use the chloroform again."

His eyes were wild and his mouth curled into an ugly snarl as he dragged her to her feet. But Luella's bonds made her stumble and only served to increase his rage.

"Move," he shouted.

"But I cannot walk – my feet are bound."

Muttering under his breath, he produced a knife from his jacket and swiftly sliced through the ropes. Luella longed to rub her sore ankles, but he was too busy dragging her out of the hut and towards the motor car.

"Get in and do not try and escape!" he screamed. "You will only come to greater harm if you do not comply with my wishes. Is that understood?"

He pulled out the gun from his jacket and pointed it at her head. Luella froze when she saw it.

"Get into the motor car and hurry!"

Luella was determined that she would not cry and tipped her head back a little to prevent the tears from flowing.

'I must be brave and do as he says,' she thought. 'There may be an opportunity once we are on the road to draw attention to my plight or to escape. I may have my hands bound, but my feet are free.'

Frank Connolly went round to the front of the Daimler and cranked the handle. It started first time much to his satisfaction.

He ceased shouting at Luella and put the gun back into his jacket pocket.

They drove back along the track and were soon on the main road. But Frank Connolly had a poor sense of direction and soon, after taking a wrong turn at a crossroads, he was hopelessly lost.

"Where are we?" he shouted at Luella.

"I don't know," she began. "I – "

"Oh, curse this! Direct me! You must know the way into Bideford."

"But I am not familiar with the roads," she insisted. "I know my way no better than you!"

"Stop talking nonsense and show me the way. If you are trying to obstruct our progress, you will be very sorry."

He fingered the gun in his pocket and Luella became very afraid of what he might do.

"T-try this way," she indicated a turning she thought looked familiar.

But they had not gone a hundred yards when the

Daimler suddenly started to splutter. It jerked and coughed before stopping completely.

"Damn! What is wrong with this infernal machine?" he shouted, his nerves now getting the better of him.

"I believe we are out of petrol," suggested Luella, who had heard Bennett describe how he had once become stranded in his previous job.

"Where can we find some?"

"I don't know. Bennett always takes care of that sort of thing."

With a furious expression he stomped back towards the passenger seat and dragged Luella out of the car.

"What are you doing?"

"Shut up! I am going to try to start it one last time."

Tying a length of rope to the bonds around her hands, he then looped it around his waist while he cranked the handle, but it was no use.

"Blasted thing! Curse it! I should have known not to trust something mechanical. I should have stolen a horse and cart – at least a horse will always go, if you give him a good-enough thrashing."

He was now utterly furious, kicking the car and using the kind of language Luella did not care to overhear.

After one last abortive attempt at starting the Daimler, the crank handle snapped in his hand. With disgust, he threw the broken metal to the ground and stamped on it.

"We will walk," he yelled hysterically.

"Where to? We are nowhere near any transport."

But Frank Connolly was not listening. He was already walking on ahead with the rope still around his waist and Luella stumbling behind him.

"This is utter folly," she pleaded, hoping to delay him. "Stop! I beg you."

"Be quiet, woman."

"What do you think you will achieve by dragging me across the country?"

"Shut up! Shut up!" he bellowed turning around to face her. He jerked the rope and she fell to the ground. Her arms ached from the motion of being led along and it took all of her strength not to cry.

"Get up. We will walk to the train station at Bideford and get on the train. Or I will hire a carriage and horses."

"You would parade me through the streets of Bideford like this?" she howled, holding up her bound hands. "Do you really think you will get away with it? Everyone knows me – they will set upon you and you will be lynched."

"Then you will have to come quietly," he snarled pulling out his pistol again. "Now shut up and walk. When the time comes, I will untie you."

Luella followed on behind him, praying with all her might that someone would see them. But the road was deserted and not a single horse or cart came along.

Eventually they reached the river. He noted with a satisfied grunt that the tide was out, so he dragged her down the steep bank to the shingle-lined shore.

"We shall be out of sight of the road this way. Now come along and do not think of giving me any trouble."

By now tears were slowly coursing down Luella's face. The sun was still warm and she was hot and thirsty. The cool water that lapped against the shingle seemed to mock her and made her even more desperate for a drink.

"Water! I must have water," she called stumbling on some pebbles.

Frank Connolly looked irritated by her request, but then he nodded.

"I don't want to have to carry you if you faint. Be quick."

He allowed Luella to walk to the water's edge and kneel down.

Putting her face into the cool water, she lapped up as much as she could before he jerked her to her feet again.

"Now get a move on. If I tie you up by the bridge, I can go and find a carriage."

"Are you mad?" asked Luella. "What if the tide comes in while I am tethered here?"

"Then at least the Viscount will not have the satisfaction of marrying you," he snapped and threw his head back with a terrifying cruel laugh.

Fear clutched at Luella's heart as they stumbled along the shore together.

'David! David. Help! Help.'

The bridge was now only a few hundred yards away and she could see he was looking for a post or one of the metal rings used by boatmen to tether their craft, so that he could strap her to it.

Suddenly, from above their heads on the bridge there came a piercing shout.

"My Lord! My Lord!"

Luella looked up to see Thomas's face staring down at her.

"It's 'er! *It's Miss Luella*! She's down on the shore."

Frank Connolly froze to the spot. He spun around and looked for somewhere to run or to hide – but there was nowhere.

Then down the set of stone steps that led from the bridge came the Viscount and a whole column of men.

"Luella!" he shouted, moving stealthily forwards with his eyes fixed firmly on Frank Connolly.

"David! *He's got a gun*!" she cried.

"And I will not hesitate to use it!" yelled Frank Connolly, as he fumbled inside his coat.

The Viscount halted in his steps as Frank Connolly drew out his pistol and, pulling Luella closer to him, he pointed it at her.

"Take one step closer and I will kill her," he hissed as his thumb flicked off the safety catch.

"What do we do now, my Lord?" whispered Thomas, as he stopped by the Viscount.

But the Viscount was not paying any attention to him or Frank Connolly. A movement up on the road had distracted his attention.

"Keep him talking," ordered the Viscount quietly.

"Very good, my Lord."

As Thomas attempted to talk Frank Connolly out of harming Luella, the Viscount moved behind him.

"Ha! Coward! Using one of your men as a shield," he roared with a triumphant look upon his face, as he pulled Luella closer to the barrel of the gun.

But the Viscount was neither a coward nor a fool. As Thomas continued to talk to him, the Viscount raised his eyes.

Up on the road, Bennett had arrived with the Police and they were creeping along the top of the river bank and down towards where Luella and Frank Connolly were standing.

Moving back in front of Thomas, the Viscount began to taunt him, hoping he would not notice the crawling men who were moving ever nearer to his rear.

"Call yourself a man," he cried. "Holding a defenceless woman prisoner. Let her go!"

"*No*! You shall not marry Luella, she is *mine*!"

"Let her go and we will fight this out, man to man. If

you win, I will not press charges, neither will Luella."

"Do you think I'm a fool?" he raged. "As soon as I let go my hold on Luella, you will have me arrested."

"You know you are doomed," parried the Viscount. "Do you really think you will escape with her and that she will go willingly with you?"

"While I have a gun pointed at her head, she has no choice."

The Viscount could see the three Policemen advancing slowly but surely behind Frank Connolly. They spread out into a triangle and moved quietly, communicating with gestures.

'I hope my men have the good sense not to alert Connolly to the fact that he is about to be captured,' thought the Viscount.

But his men were used to hunting and the pursuit of quarry. They stood stock-still and not even their eyes moved an inch from Frank Connolly's face.

'I have them rapt,' he thought triumphantly, as he began to drag Luella towards the bridge steps.

"Let me pass and she will not be harmed," he demanded.

But no sooner had the words left his lips than three Policemen closed in on him from behind.

One grabbed the hand that held the gun and deftly prised it from his grip, while the other two pulled him to the ground.

Luella fell forward and the Viscount rushed towards her.

"My darling!" he cried taking her in his arms and kissing her over and over again. "Are you hurt?"

"A little," whimpered Luella. "But I am alive and that is all that matters. Oh, David! I thought I would be killed –

or worse – *and he was going to shoot you too.*"

He cradled her tenderly in his arms and kissed her face. Luella closed her eyes and sighed as his lips sought her eyelids and her mouth.

The Viscount did not care if everyone was staring.

All that mattered was that Luella was safe.

*

Frank Connolly was taken to Bideford Police station and charged with attempted abduction and plotting to murder the Viscount.

When the Chief Constable telephoned the Viscount later that evening to check that Luella was well, he assured him that Connolly was safely locked up in the cells at the station.

"And he will not be allowed to go free. You have my word on that, my Lord."

"Excellent, Chief Constable. I will, of course, be prepared to give evidence. I just hope that the trial will not clash with my forthcoming marriage."

"Of course, my Lord. He will be charged in the morning and a date will be set for the trial. He will not see the light of day for a very long time, I can assure you. Kidnap is enough to send him down for many years without the intent to murder in addition."

"Splendid, I will inform Luella. She will be glad that she is now free of the scourge of Frank Connolly."

The Viscount replaced the receiver and made his way upstairs to the blue room. Grace was sitting outside as the doctor was tending to Luella.

"How is Miss Ridgeway?" he asked Grace as he paused outside the door.

"She is very tired, my Lord, but glad to be home. She has been through a terrible ordeal – terrible!"

"Yes, indeed she has."

He knocked on the door and waited for the doctor to answer.

"Ah, my Lord," he called. "Please come in. Miss Ridgeway is resting."

"Is she – ?"

"She is untouched, my Lord."

"Then that is something to be grateful for. Will there be any ill-effects from her ordeal?"

"She is still a little disorientated after inhaling so much chloroform. She can expect a bad headache, but a few good nights sleep should see her as right as rain."

"May I see her?"

"Yes, but I warn you, she is very tired. Do not stay long, as she needs rest."

The Viscount thanked the doctor, shook his hand and entered the room.

Luella was in bed with her tanned hands folded over the coverlet. Her thick golden hair was loose and spread out across the pillow and the Viscount thought she looked for all the world like an angel sent down from Heaven.

"David? Is that you?"

"Yes, my love. I am here."

He rushed to the bed and took her hands in his, kissing them gently.

"I have sent Grace downstairs to bring you something to eat. Do you think you can manage it?"

Seeing her pale face turned up to his, his heart melted. She had never looked lovelier and he was seized with the desire to crush her in his arms.

"Thank you, darling," she murmured sinking back into the pillow. "I am so tired I do not know how I can keep my eyes open, but the doctor has ordered me to keep my strength up so I will try to eat whatever Grace brings me."

"Good. Your tiredness is due to the shock taking effect. The doctor also mentioned something about chloroform?"

"Yes, Frank Connolly put me to sleep with it in the garden. That is how he abducted me."

"I feel sick at the thought of his filthy hands all over you."

"We must forget about him," implored Luella wearily. "He is the past now. We have nothing more to fear from him."

Just then Grace came into the room carrying a tray. The Viscount bade Luella goodbye and returned downstairs.

As he reached the foot of the stairs, he remembered that his motor car was abandoned somewhere. He rang for Bennett and charged him to take a cart out to where Luella had said it had broken down and retrieve it.

"You should take some petrol with you, Miss Luella believes that is why it stopped."

"Of course, she is right, my Lord. As I told you, I had not the chance to fill the car before Connolly stole it. This is one occasion when it was fortunate that I decided to have tea before I went out to the barn, my Lord. Had I filled the Daimler up, Connolly might be miles away by now!"

"Yes, it does not bear thinking about," sighed the Viscount. "We should all give thanks to Our Lord for saving her."

As Bennett left the hall, the Viscount's lips moved in prayer. With his hand on his heart, he spoke to his mother in Heaven, feeling certain she had been watching over him and Luella.

'Mama, I almost lost her,' he whispered. 'If I did not

know how much I loved her before, then now I realise she is the most precious thing on earth to me. *Thank you for saving her.*'

With his head bowed, he took a deep breath and made his way to the library.

Nearly losing Luella had made him realise how much he missed his father.

'I would give anything to be reconciled with him and for him to attend my wedding,' he muttered as he sat down at his desk to write a letter.

*

Luella slept solidly for the next few days, but by the end of the week she was well enough to get up and sit in the new conservatory to read a book.

The builders were making great progress and the new wing was almost ready to move into. Luella kept away from the work, as the after-effects of the chloroform meant that her throat was still sore and it would only be aggravated by dust.

Grace had just brought her some lemon-barley water when she heard the front door bell ring.

"Are we expecting visitors?" she asked. "I have not forgotten about a dress fitting, have I?"

"No, miss. I specifically telephoned the dressmaker and told her not to come this week as you were indisposed. I cannot imagine that it is her."

Luella returned to her book, only to be interrupted again – this time by Cork.

"Miss Ridgeway, would you come to the drawing room? You have a visitor."

"But, Cork, you know that I am not at home to anyone who calls."

"Begging your pardon, miss, but I think you will want

to see this particular visitor."

'Who on earth can it be?' wondered Luella, as she rose to walk downstairs.

She put down her book with a sigh and thought the whole affair a great nuisance.

But upon entering the drawing room, she let out a cry of delight as there, in the middle of the carpet, stood Aunt Edith.

"Aunt," she cried. "How wonderful to see you. What on earth brings you back from Scotland so soon? I told you we could manage with the wedding preparations – "

Cork coughed behind her and Aunt Edith looked at him expectantly.

"Cork?" she said enigmatically.

"I shall go and fetch his Lordship at once, my Lady. If you care to wait here."

"Are you not staying, Aunt?" asked Luella thoroughly mystified. "Where are your cases?"

"Wait until David gets here."

"Then, you must take a seat at least."

"I will stand," she answered, leaving Luella perplexed by her behaviour.

A few moments later, the Viscount strode into the drawing room .

"Lady Ridgeway. What a wonderful surprise. What brings you back to Devon?"

The Countess smiled and took his arm.

"Now, I want you to come out to my carriage, David," she started.

"What the – "

"No arguments, David. Come with me."

Luella moved to follow them.

"Alone, please," said Aunt Edith firmly, much to Luella's astonishment.

The Viscount shook his head believing that the Countess had quite taken leave of her senses, but he humoured her and allowed her to lead him to the front door.

Outside stood her carriage with its team of huge grey horses and its black coachwork gleamed in the sunshine.

'Perhaps she has a present for Luella that she does not wish her to see,' thought the Viscount.

But as he looked up, a top-hatted figure appeared in the carriage window.

At first, he did not recognise the man. Then, not quite believing his eyes, the Viscount stood frozen to the spot while the footman opened the carriage door.

"Hello, David."

Climbing down the steps towards him was his father!

The Viscount let out a cry of delight and a flood of emotion swept through his body as he took in his father's warm expression.

"*Father*! What a surprise?" he exclaimed, swallowing the lump in his throat.

"Are you going to invite me inside?" said the Earl with a smile. "And I think you will find there is someone else inside the carriage who is eager to see you."

The Viscount stepped eagerly forward and held his breath as he reached the carriage steps –

CHAPTER TEN

"Hello, David," came a familiar voice.

The Viscount's emotions swelled inside him as he spied the face of his beloved grandmother. She smiled warmly at him from her seat in the carriage.

"*Grandmama!*" he cried. "You have come. When I sent that last letter – "

"It was not your grandmother's idea to come here," interrupted the Earl. "It was mine. Well, are you not going to invite us inside?"

The Viscount's mouth dropped open.

"Why, of course."

"And help your grandmother down those steps. She is not as nimble on her feet as she once was and the Countess's carriage has steeper steps than ours."

Taking his grandmother's arm, the Viscount helped her down and escorted her into the house.

She looked around wistfully as they entered the hall with its oak staircase and panelled walls.

"It is magnificent," she breathed, as she viewed the stag's head on the wall over the stairwell. "I did not imagine – "

"That you would ever set foot in this house," finished the Viscount, as she began to walk forward leaning on his arm.

"No."

"I must confess I am a little surprised to see you here, Grandmama. I would have thought that what with the house's history – "

"And it is just that – history," she replied firmly. "We should all remember that."

The Viscount patted her hand and led her to the drawing room where he knew Luella was waiting for them.

She gasped as she saw the Viscount enter the room with the old lady on his arm. She guessed at once who it was.

"Madam. You have come at last," she cried moving forward to kiss her.

"You must be Luella," she said with a smile. "I am sorry I did not reply to your letter. We were in Biarritz and I only received it last week. And then the Countess came to see us and it seemed a propitious time to visit."

"Aunt Edith?" exclaimed Luella. "You went to see David's grandmother?"

"Yes, my dear, I did. And I hope you will forgive me for being so interfering, but there is someone else here too who would very much like to meet you."

A look of bewilderment crossed Luella's face.

"I am not all alone," interjected the Dowager Marchioness.

Luella looked over to the doorway of the drawing room to see a rather distinguished-looking man handing his top hat to Cork. He bore more than a passing resemblance to the Viscount. There was something about the strong jaw and resolute pose – and Luella could not quite believe her eyes.

"Luella, this is my father, the Earl of Kennington," announced the Viscount, as he strode towards Luella with a smile.

"My dear, I can see *exactly* why my son has chosen you for his bride."

He took her hand and kissed it. Luella remained speechless, such was her state of shock at meeting David's father.

"Ever since the Countess told us about you, I have longed to meet you and you are every bit as beautiful as she described you," he said with shining eyes. "She came to see us, you know. To tell us about your wedding."

Luella threw a glance towards Aunt Edith who was smiling broadly.

"I was wrong, David," continued the Earl, as he stood before his son. "And it took the Countess here to make me see the error of my ways. What she said made me realise that I did not wish to remain estranged from you and especially now that you are to be married. I did not wish to be a stranger to any grandchildren that may come along. You are, after all, my only son."

"Papa!" choked the Viscount, his voice trembling with emotion. "I am so glad to see you both. I cannot tell you how happy this will make us. Having you both attend our wedding means such a great deal."

Luella helped the Dowager Marchioness to a comfortable chair and rang for Cork to bring refreshments.

"You must be tired after your long journey. You came all the way in Aunt Edith's carriage?"

"We did. I did not wish to have to change trains at Exeter and besides it gave us the opportunity to stop over at Salisbury to pay a visit to my old friend, the Duchess of Trowbridge."

The Viscount rushed forward to his grandmother and knelt beside her.

"Grandmama, I still cannot believe you are here!"

"In the house where my husband defiled our wedding vows, you mean?" she asserted in a loud clear voice. "David, I can see that you have great plans for this house. Edith has told us of your improvements and soon it will no longer be a place to avoid, but a house full of love, laughter and, I hope, children."

The Viscount kissed her hand and looked over to where Luella and her aunt were sitting both crying tears of joy.

"Such a day I thought I would never see," he murmured. "To have you in my house and to be reconciled with Papa means so much to me."

The Earl moved over to where Luella was sitting and took her hands.

"I hope you will not think so ill of me and my past behaviour that I will not be welcome at your wedding," he said. "And if you still wish to wed here and not in London, then I will not object."

"Our day would not be complete without you to give me away," suggested Luella. "My own dear Papa is dead and I do not have another male relative I could ask. Would you do me the honour?"

The Earl blushed and appeared deeply moved by her request. He was too overcome to speak, but simply nodded and squeezed her hands.

At that moment, Cork and Mrs. Cork entered, carrying trays of tea and cakes.

The Viscount waved them away saying,

"Never mind tea, I think champagne is in order."

"My Lord, I have some on ice in the kitchen. I anticipated it might be required," said Cork with a smile.

"Well, I would like tea *and* champagne," declared the Countess.

Mrs. Cork soon obliged and, as Cork returned with a magnum of the finest champagne, the Earl proposed a toast.

"To Luella and David," he suggested, raising his glass to the ceiling. "May they both be happy and enjoy a wonderful future together."

"To Luella and David!" echoed the Dowager Marchioness and the Countess.

The Viscount moved closer to Luella and put his arm around her, moving her as he did so towards the French doors that led into the gardens.

"Darling," he whispered in her ear, as they stepped outside. "I have a confession to make. I wrote to Grandmama and told her of our engagement, but I can see that it was your aunt who tipped the scales in our favour."

"And your father is here!"

"That will be Grandmama's doing. Papa, stubborn as he might be, will always eventually come around to her way of thinking. He loves her a great deal and I can see now that he was only trying to protect her."

"I did not realise – "

"That the house belonged to Grandpapa's mistress? Yes, even I did not know of her existence until it came to the reading of the will. It is not something I wished to discuss and I never thought I would see the day that Grandmama came here."

"But she has," murmured Luella. "She is a very wise woman. Darling, history should not harm us, it is dead while we are very much alive. And I am certain that Madame Le Fevre, wherever she is in Heaven, would not wish to come between two young lovers."

"You are right. The French are so much more adept at matters of the heart than we British," replied the Viscount. "Now, come. We should return to the drawing room and join the celebrations."

"Aunt Edith is a wonder, is she not?"

"She is, indeed. I can see that she has made a great impression on Grandmama already and that is no easy task."

*

The Earl and the Dowager Marchioness stayed until after luncheon before leaving to find a hotel in Bideford where they could stay until the day of the wedding.

The Viscount offered rooms at Torr House, but his grandmother declined, saying that she would find it difficult to sleep with the builders starting so early each day.

The Viscount knew that really it was not the idea of the builders she found difficult, but sleeping under what had once been Madame Le Fevre's roof.

As he waved them off, he noticed a buggy coming up the drive.

He squinted into the distance and, eventually, made out the figure of the Chief Constable seated alongside another Police Officer.

The buggy came to a halt outside and the Chief Constable climbed down.

"Chief Constable. What brings you here?"

"Might we go inside?" he said. "It is a rather delicate matter."

The Viscount showed him into the library where they would not be disturbed.

"Would you care for some refreshment? I am afraid I am a little less than sober and would like some coffee, if you would care to join me?"

"Thank you, my Lord. Although you may wish for something stronger after I have told you what I came to say."

"Oh?"

"It's Frank Connolly."

"You have a date for the trial?"

"I'm afraid he has now dispensed with the need for a trial."

"I do not understand, Chief Constable. How can he have done such a thing? Has his father pulled some strings high up?"

The Chief Constable shifted in his seat and looked uncomfortable.

"My Lord, we found him hanging by his necktie in his cell this morning. Frank Connolly is dead."

The Viscount fell back in his chair utterly shocked.

"My God!" he exclaimed. "He really was not of sound mind. Did he leave a note?"

"No, but you are correct in assuming that his mind was touched."

"I must say, although I detested the fellow, I would not have wished this for him. Still, I suppose it spares Luella the pain of a trial. She would have found it difficult to bear having to see that man again. Have you informed his father?"

"Yes, we telephoned him in Ireland as soon as he was discovered. He is on his way here to collect the body."

"It is a great shame for his family. I do not personally know the Connollys of Kilsharry, but they do not deserve this terrible stain on their good name."

The Chief Constable drained his cup and rose to leave.

"Will you inform Miss Ridgeway?"

"Yes, at once."

"Then, I'll bid you good afternoon, my Lord. I am sorry to bring such bad news to this house at a time when it should be filled with joy. Do not worry about having me shown out, I know the way."

The Viscount remained in his chair and sighed deeply.

Although he was relieved that Frank Connolly would never cast a shadow over him or Luella again, he was not untouched by the tragedy of the affair.

'Luella will be upset and will blame herself,' he murmured. 'I must make certain that she realises that he was not in his right mind and that men in such desperate situations are wont to take desperate action.'

He rose to find Luella, his heart heavy and full of dread at what her reaction might be.

*

Much to the Viscount's surprise, Luella took the news of Frank Connolly's self-inflicted demise without becoming too distressed.

She simply sighed and said that it was a great pity that he should have taken his own life. But she was relieved to be spared the prospect of reliving the awful events of the past and refused to allow it to cloud their happiness.

The Earl and the Dowager Marchioness remained in Bideford. Luella was delighted that the old lady took an active part in the preparations alongside her Aunt Edith, while the Viscount found his father to be an enthusiastic partner, helping him ensure that the building work on Torr House was completed in record time.

He even paid for more builders and craftsmen to come from London so that the house would be ready in time for the celebrations.

On the day of the wedding, the Viscount went to stay in the same hotel as his family, while Luella and her aunt remained at Torr House.

Grace was in a high state of excitement as she woke Luella early on that late September morning.

The wedding dress was hanging from the wardrobe in the river room and was the first thing that Luella saw as she opened her eyes.

'Today, I am to become *Lady Kennington,*' she said to herself with mounting excitement.

She climbed out of bed and Grace drew her a bath. After the ceremony, Luella would be moving into the rooms in the new wing with the Viscount.

'Tonight I shall not say goodnight to him and be apart from him,' she mused as she lay back in the steaming water. 'I shall lie in his arms and we shall become one in our love.'

She suddenly wished that her mother was with her to advise her and to allay her fears. By the time that Grace began to brush out her thick golden hair, Luella was feeling upset that her parents were no longer around to see her big day.

Seeing her Mistress close to tears, Grace made an excuse to leave the room and ran to where the Countess was breakfasting in the conservatory.

"Grace, what is it?"

The Countess saw the worried expression on the maid's face and knew at once that she had come about Luella.

"It is Miss Luella. She is very upset and I think she needs you by her side."

The Countess set down her toast and followed Grace upstairs.

Luella was hunched over the dressing table crying profusely. With a slight gesture the Countess dismissed Grace and went over to her niece embracing her warmly.

"Darling, what is it?"

"I just wish so much that Mama and Papa were alive to witness this day. I would so love Mama to be here with me."

"You must miss them very much. We all do, but today of all days it will seem as if the proceedings are somehow lacking without them. Am I right?"

"As ever, Aunt Edith. Don't think I am not grateful for your being here – you have always been as a mother to me, but this day would have meant a great deal to Mama."

"And to my brother-in-law, your father," sighed the Countess.

Luella clutched the photograph of her parents that always stood on the dressing table firmly to her bosom.

"It is as if a piece of my heart died with them."

"Yes, I do understand, darling. But you know that you owe it to them and their memory to be happy on this day. They would not want you crying and miserable."

Luella looked at the photograph and kissed it.

"Of course, Aunt Edith. That is how it should be, but I do so wish that they could see me getting married. It is just that David reconciling with his father has made me long for my parents to be here too. They would love David, as I do."

"But they will see you. From Heaven."

"I wish I could believe it. I would feel so much better if I thought they could watch me and be smiling down on me today."

"They will. You must look into your heart and find the truth. God will show you the way, my dear. Pray to Him and He will send you their love through Him."

Luella dried her eyes and nodded. She clasped her hands together and said a silent prayer, hoping with all her heart that she would be heard.

"I feel much better now," she announced, as Grace tiptoed back into the room. "Aunt, thank you so much. I do not know what I would do without your wisdom."

"Darling, we have all loved and lost dear ones and on days like this they are always with us."

The Countess quietly left her to her preparations.

As Luella stepped into her wedding dress, a beam of sunlight suddenly struck her dress as she moved towards the mirror.

Gasping in wonder, she said to herself,

"*It is a sign*! A sign that Mama and Papa are with me."

Feeling comforted, Luella's spirits soared and soon she found herself in the carriage seated next to the Earl on her way to the Church. Joy in her heart at last.

*

The ceremony went without a hitch and everyone who attended agreed that Luella was the most beautiful and radiant bride that Bideford, if not the whole of England, had ever seen.

The Viscount, so dashing and handsome in his morning suit led her down the aisle after they had been pronounced man and wife, and felt filled with joy that his father and grandmother had been present to witness the happiest moment in his life.

Bennett had the Daimler waiting for them and had decorated it with white ribbons. The whole of Bideford thronged the churchyard and cheered them on as they emerged from the Church.

Rice and confetti showered them from every angle as they walked towards the motor car.

As the Daimler sped them towards Torr House, Luella nestled close to her new husband and sent a silent prayer of thanks to God for her good fortune.

The Viscount looked at her as she cast her eyes downwards and thought that he was so happy he might burst.

"Luella," he murmured gently raising her face to his. "Until I met you, I did not realise the importance of love. And now I know that, without love, we do not live – we simply exist."

She smiled back up at him, her eyes full of warmth and deep affection.

"Oh, my darling, I thought I would never find a man who would love me after that awful business with Jean-Marie Bouillicault, let alone anyone as wonderful as you."

The Viscount leaned in towards her and kissed her on the lips. As they kissed, people in the street cheered and waved.

Back at Torr House, he led her inside and took her in his arms as they stood on the front steps.

A cavalcade of carriages was coming down the drive towards them and Luella realised that this was their last chance of privacy before the house filled with guests, eagerly awaiting the wedding breakfast.

"My dearest darling," she whispered fluttering her eyelashes and gazing up at him. "I want to be the very best wife you could ever wish for."

Filled with passion the Viscount kissed her again.

He could feel her heart beating and her pulse racing as he traced the line of her neck with his fingers.

"Come," he said at last. "Our guests are arriving. Let us go inside and drink a toast to *us*."

"And to *love*," sighed Luella allowing him to lead her inside.

And to a world of happiness and delight for all Eternity.

To a life together of tenderness and gentleness.

To a life of unending bliss.